A BRIDE FOR

CW00730073

By marrying Pip, Hallam Fielding would gain a
clinic nurse, a general secretary, cook, housekeeper and slave—and all for free! Knowing this,
Pip still could not resist him. Even if he could
never love her, was it sufficient if she could
somehow make him want her?

A BRIDE FOR THE SURGEON

BY

HAZEL FISHER

MILLS & BOON LIMITED
London · Sydney · Toronto

First published in Great Britain 1981
by Mills & Boon Limited,
15–16 Brook's Mews,
London W1A 1DR

© Hazel Fisher 1981

Australian copyright 1981
Philippine copyright 1981

ISBN 0 263 73717 9

Set in Monophoto Times 11 on 11½ pt.

Made and printed in Great Britain by
Richard Clay (The Chaucer Press) Ltd,
Bungay, Suffolk

CHAPTER ONE

NERVOUSLY, Philippa Weston twisted her mother's wedding ring round and round her middle finger, then stared down at it, unseeingly.

Behind the massive desk, Hallam Fielding re-read Pip's letter of application. It gave her a moment to study his lean features, more to take her mind off the ordeal than for any other reason. The straight dark hair was greying at the temples, and it receded a little, showing his high forehead to advantage. The nose was just right, she decided, neither too big nor too small, the chin firm and determined, adding character to his handsome face. But his mouth was a hard, straight line. A cruel mouth, she was thinking, when those dark, storm-grey eyes focussed on her again.

She felt hot colour creep up her face, feeling that, all the time, he had been aware of her scrutiny.

'You seem to have had a lot of jobs in your young life, Miss Weston,' he shot at her.

'Have I?' Pip asked, warily. 'I have been with Mrs Noakes for nearly a year.'

'A year might seem a long time to someone of your tender years,' he acknowledged, dropping his eyes again, 'but it seems rather short to me.'

Her generous mouth tightened, and she had a hard fight to keep back the words of protest. Remember, she told herself, you don't need this job but Melanie and Simon need the flat that goes with it. *They* haven't anywhere else to go. It was

5

only that thought that kept her from telling the autocratic surgeon exactly what he was, as the inquisition went on.

Why had she given up her general nurse training? Why, with such good 'O' level results, hadn't she stayed on at school, gone to university? Why did she want a job with accommodation?

She answered as truthfully as she could, all the while feeling she was a prisoner in the dock, defending herself while the lawyer for the prosecution sharpened his teeth on her. She had given up her training when her mother became ill with a terminal illness, and had nursed her until she died. University had never appealed to her as she had wanted to nurse since childhood. As she had no home of her own, naturally a living-in position was preferable.

'It's far better than a dreary bed-sit,' she told him, firmly, but he seemed not to hear.

While Mr Fielding silently debated the matter, Pip's blue eyes swept over the study. It was small but cosy. Behind the large desk was an equally massive swivel chair where Mr Fielding sat. Small gilt chairs with embroidered seats, obviously antique, were spread around the room, and Pip didn't find the one on which she was sitting at all comfortable. Book-shelves filled one wall, and she perked up a little. Books were her special love, and if they were nursing textbooks, so much the better. Wide-eyed, she glanced at the gilt clock just behind the surgeon's left shoulder. Twenty to five. Her appointment had been for three o'clock but her prospective employer had been delayed by an emergency.

The housekeeper who had let her in had asked if

Pip wanted to come back later to save a long wait, and Pip had shaken her head decisively. No, she would wait. She must wait, for if she left she knew she wouldn't have the courage, the sheer gall to come back to offer her services to Hallam Fielding, the well-known surgeon.

He required a general help for his private practice, someone with nursing experience to stand in for his usual nurse, a companion for his Aunt Norah, a social secretary-cum-typist ... and cum-everything else, Pip decided in dismay. And rumour had it he wasn't prepared to pay much. The man was a slave-driver, an ogre.

'Will you continue your training at some time?' he said, at last. Those eyes transfixed her and she felt like a butterfly being nailed to the board. She trembled slightly, hoping he wouldn't notice.

'I expect so,' she said quietly, wondering if she ever would. Perhaps when Melanie's problem was settled ...

'How long could I expect you to stay here then?' he wanted to know, and she hesitated, unsure of the answer herself.

'I don't know, Mr Fielding,' she admitted. 'I certainly don't plan to re-start my training for the next two or three years.' That should give Melanie ample time to get settled. 'Perhaps not at all. Things are ... are difficult at the moment.'

'Ah! Boyfriend trouble?' He raised a heavy brow.

She had time to notice that his brows met in the middle, before she shook her head. 'Not exactly.' Eyebrows that met in the middle were a sure sign of a violent temper, she'd heard.

'Oh, married, is he?' He looked down at her letter again, disapproval in every line of him.

Yes, he's married! she wanted to scream at him. He's my sister's husband. It's *her* trouble, not mine!

Mr Fielding was a hateful, prudish man, she decided unfairly, and he could keep his job.

'I have had twenty-nine applications for this post, Miss Weston,' he said, suddenly.

'Oh!' She couldn't keep the sadness from her voice. There was certainly no hope for her now, so it was a good thing she had decided against the post anyway, wasn't it? She studied her hands. So Melanie would have to find somewhere else. Out here, in the heart of the country, would have been so suitable . . .

'Twenty-four of them have a dependent child,' he went on, 'and the other four each have an elderly parent who would, otherwise, be dumped in a Home or in some dreary bed-sit, as you mentioned earlier.'

Mutely, she nodded. Poor old biddies. 'Naturally, you must give the job to one of them,' she agreed, then added hastily, at the frosty look bestowed on her: 'I mean, I do understand that they *need* the accommodation provided with this post.'

'I do not run a charity, Miss Weston!' he snapped, clearly at the end of his tether. 'Whether they need the accommodation or not is hardly re-levant. Would they make efficient secretaries is the criterion, surely?'

'Yes, of course,' she agreed, miserably. Every word she said was making things worse. She knew she could make a success of the job but could hardly say so. What was the use of trying? This man had obviously made up his mind that she was totally unsuitable so why didn't he get it over with? A quick, clean cut and it would all be over.

If only Melanie wasn't relying on the application being successful! Pip had almost made up her mind to fling the job back in the consultant's face, but memory came unbidden of her sister's trusting gaze. Melanie's eyes were a paler blue than Pip's, her hair, unlike Pip's which was red-gold, was almost honey-blonde, soft and shining, or was when she had time and the inclination to attend to it. For the past few months Melanie had taken little interest in her appearance. She was depressed—and becoming even more estranged from her husband, Peter. She had married very young and now, still only nineteen, had a young son, Simon. She and Peter had been drifting apart and she'd begged Pip to find a job with accommodation, so that she and Simon could live with Pip, just for a while, perhaps, to give Melanie and Peter a breathing space; to enable them to decide what they really wanted from their marriage.

Pip's soft heart was no match for Melanie's tears, her almost constant tales of woe. Yes, she would leave Mrs Noakes's employ, answer the advertisement Melanie had thrust under her nose, try to make a home for the three of them, temporarily.

The job was certainly nothing to rush for, with probably long hours and low wages, but the advertisement had contained the magic words—'Flat in grounds for successful applicant. Child not objected to.'

'That's it!' Melanie had called, excitedly. 'Simon and I can come and live with you!'

Pip had carefully pointed out that the child Mr Fielding envisaged would be a school-age one, a child who did not need constant attention, but Melanie, bright-eyed and eager for once, had brushed the objections aside. The three of them would live together. It would be like old times, she'd insisted and, as always, Pip hadn't the heart to refuse. Poor Melanie was a soft-hearted girl, perhaps too immature to bear the strains and stresses of married life. But she was mature enough to decide she needed a change of venue to enable her to get her problems in perspective, so of course Pip would leave her pleasant, if slightly dull, post as Mrs Noakes's companion. Of course Pip would try to get a job with suitable accommodation. Melanie had hugged her, so had little Simon. Somehow the sacrifice all seemed worthwhile at the time. But now . . .

'Give me one good reason why I should give you the post, Miss Weston,' he barked at her, and she jumped, visibly shaken. Then her eyes met his, deep blue ones being forced to yield by stormy-grey, and she rebelled.

She would *not* be browbeaten! She had been kicked around as a child, she would not allow this so-superior person to call the tune! 'I can't think of a good reason, Mr Fielding,' she said, firmly, trading stares with him. 'But you could give me a trial,' she hurried on, before her courage deserted her. 'I'm sure I would be satisfactory.' There, that was telling him!

Twin spots of colour appeared on her cheeks, and she could feel them burning, but she refused to look away. His eyes were boring into her very soul but she would not be the first one to drop her gaze. She was determined on that.

A reluctant smile touched the thin mouth briefly,

but never reached his eyes. 'A lady of spirit,' he commented. He leant back in the chair and crossed his long legs.

The cold eyes never left her face, and she felt a strange excitement, mingled with apprehension. The job, if he offered it, would be a challenge and so would this man. She found herself eager to take on both, for her own sake as well as for her sister's.

Something of her eagerness must have shown on her face, because Hallam Fielding nodded slowly, as if he'd finally made up his mind.

'Very well. You can have the position, Miss Weston. On one month's trial,' he went on, warningly, as she leant forward, eyes shining. 'If,' he continued, sternly, 'you are still unsatisfactory at the end of that time, you go. Just like that!' He snapped his fingers, and she flinched.

Determination in every inch of her, she said: 'I won't be unsatisfactory! I'm sure you will let me stay on!'

'That, Miss Weston, I very much doubt,' he said, voice heavy with sarcasm. 'I doubt that you will last one week, let alone one month, but we shall see.' He rose, towering over her. Hurriedly, she got up too, and stared up at him, not to be outdone just because he was a good foot taller.

'Come on, I'll show you the flat. *That* is what interests you about the job, isn't it?' Without waiting for a reply, he strode from the room, and her legs couldn't keep pace with him. She found herself running to keep up, and knew it was what he wanted. He intended to humiliate her, make her feel inferior, smaller than she actually was. He was arrogant, insufferable ... Certainly if it hadn't been for Melanie she would not have borne his taunts without retaliation.

Hallam Fielding had crossed the yard by the time Pip got to the back-door of his house. He was about to enter what seemed like a stable, and her spirits fell. Surely she hadn't to live over a horse-box?

It hadn't dawned on her, or on Melanie, that the accommodation might be unsuitable for a small child. Simon was still an infant, susceptible to infection, still testing anything new by putting it in his mouth. Goodness knows what he would pick up there!

Why, it must be some kind of potato-loft! she decided. Once, as a child of ten, she'd visited her Aunt Nellie in Leicestershire and spent a few happy precious days playing in Aunt Nellie's potato-loft. She still recalled with pleasure the sweet smell, the warmth. But it didn't mean she wanted to live in one now!

He beckoned imperiously, and Pip hurried across the paved yard to the tall building opposite.

'This used to be the chauffeur's accommodation when some wealthy big-wig lived here,' he explained, as she gazed dubiously at the building.

She could see now that it was a barn used as a garage. Mr Fielding's Rolls-Royce stood in state in the middle of the barn, next to a bright green sports-car. His wife's, perhaps? Where was the flat, then?

'The entrance is around here. Come on,' he said, testily, as she seemed inclined to linger over the Rolls. She had never seen such a splendid car in close-up before.

The flat wasn't, after all, above the garage but

was attached to it. It had a separate entrance, and, meekly, she followed Mr Fielding up the steps.

She counted thirteen, and shuddered. Thirteen steps to the gallows, wasn't it? Whatever it was, she was far too sensible to be superstitious, she hoped!

When he pushed open the unlocked door, she exclaimed, in delight: 'Oh, it's cosy! Just like a home should be!'

Forgetting him entirely, she scurried from room to room running her hands over almost everything. True, it was small but . . . but it looked so homely. Just what she'd imagined her longed-for cottage in the country would be like.

The front-door opened directly into the sitting-room, a poky but bright room. On one side was the kitchenette, L-shaped and very narrow, but made to appear more spacious by clever use of white and by the compact units. A window ran the length of the kitchen and, eagerly, she ran to in-spect the view. Roses! How perfect! Would Simon be allowed in the garden? she wondered, then realised in horror that she hadn't mentioned him.

Melanie had suggested she pass off Simon as her own, invent a dead fiancé or something, but Pip had been adamant about that. She would not lie to the man, yet somehow she had to bring the child—and Melanie—into the conversation.

'Something not right about the view, Miss Weston?' He was only inches from her and he looked so big and fierce, as if he ate red-heads for dinner.

Pip was more than a little afraid of him but didn't intend to show it. 'I love roses,' she said. Unconsciously, her expression took on the proud, defiant quality Hallam was beginning to find so charming, but he merely nodded.

'Good. When you've seen the bedrooms and usual offices, I will show you where you actually work.'

His emphasis on the last word wasn't lost on Pip, and she hurried to inspect the bedrooms. There were two of them, to her delight. True, one was very tiny indeed, no more than a junk-room, but it would do for her. Melanie and Simon must have the bigger room. Both were simply furnished with single beds, a chest of drawers and a chair. The larger room boasted a double wardrobe and dressing-table as well, so they would manage. They had few clothes between them. Melanie hadn't had any new clothes for ages and Pip never bothered. In any case, her brother-in-law wasn't overfond of work and Pip often slipped a few pounds to Melanie to buy something for the little boy.

She clenched her fists, longing to have the shiftless Peter Elliott in her power, just for a moment.

'When you have finished scowling at the bedroom, perhaps we could get along.' The cold voice snapped her back to reality. Had she really been scowling?

'I'm sorry,' she said, faintly. 'It's a very pleasant room. I was thinking of something else.'

He grunted, which could have meant anything, and hurried down the steps again and was at his back-door while Pip was still halfway down.

'Nurses generally hurry, Miss Weston. Surely you remember?'

'I'm out of practice, Mr Fielding. Mrs Noakes didn't expect me to scurry about for no reason!' she retorted, then stopped, aghast. Her eyes opened wide with dismay at her rudeness.

Hallam Fielding stared as if he couldn't quite believe his ears. Then, shrugging as if the irritation named Pip Weston was of no account, he led the way to a big, sunny room at the side of the house. 'This is where you will work.' He waved a hand expansively, then stood aside while she explored like an eager puppy.

An electric typewriter! Luxury, indeed. Of course, she had never used an electric one before, but probably there wasn't much difference between it and a manual one.

'I see your typing speed is sixty,' he said, quietly. 'Is that adequate?'

She spun round. 'Oh, it's a very good speed!' she assured him, then went to inspect the cupboards, and was unaware of the smile that lit up the surgeon's lean features.

The cupboards were filled with stationery, as she would expect, but one contained nursing equipment and her eyes lit up. And textbooks! Lovingly, she ran her hands over the books. It seemed years since she'd started her general training. Oh, would she ever be able to go back? She had stayed with Mrs Noakes so as to be near Melanie, but had intended to resume training shortly. But now . . .

'You can read them in your off-duty.'

Eyes alight with pleasure, she beamed at him, her rather plain little face becoming almost beautiful for a moment.

Hallam smothered a groan and turned it into a cough, instead. What had possessed him to give this girl the job? He was a fool, an *old* fool, and she was just a child. Yet she had talked back at him, defied him—and enchanted him.

Reflectively, he ran long, surgeon's fingers over the stubble on his chin. He ought to have shaved again. Damn the girl! Damn all women!

Puzzled, Pip waited while her new employer brought his feelings under control. She felt she had upset him again, but couldn't think how. He was certainly going to be *very* hard to please!

'Aunt Norah is away at present but should be back in a day or so.'

Pip nodded. Yes, Aunt Norah would be another hurdle to face. She licked her lips, not wanting to say the wrong thing again. 'Do you ... I mean, how is she to get along with? Your Aunt Norah?'

'Crabby,' he said, succinctly.

'Oh!' Dismay was written all over her face. 'She can't be that crabby, surely? I expect she has everything she needs.' How could anyone be dissatisfied with such a gorgeous house and money?

'She is *that* crabby' the surgeon assured her, eyes gleaming with what might have been malice. 'Even if I find your work satisfactory, Aunt Norah will not, so you had better make your mind up to stay only the month! Perhaps you should read the situations vacant column during that time!' was his parting shot, before he disappeared into what he'd said were his consulting rooms.

Hands on hips, Pip glared, but he was already gone. Nasty so-and-so! He didn't *want* her to succeed, but she intended to. She would tame Hallam Fielding as well as his Aunt Norah!

Tentatively, she peeked around the door of the consulting rooms. Stainless-steel units, a washbasin, couches, screens. She wrinkled her small nose, believing she could smell that evocative *hospital* smell.

Another door opened on the other side, and she walked towards it, across a lino-tiled floor. The whole room was bigger than her flat, she decided.

The adjoining room was the consultant's study, where the interview had taken place. Mr Fielding perched on the edge of a small table, while he thumbed through a desk-diary.

Pip edged nearer, uncertain of his temper. She would give as good as she got, but there was absolutely no point in starting an argument if it could be avoided. Remember Melanie and Simon, she told herself.

'When can you start?' he shot at her, and she halted in her tracks, brow wrinkled in thought.

'Mrs Noakes is fully recovered now and says I can leave anytime,' she assured him, voice wobbling a little. She liked old Mrs Noakes and would have been perfectly content to remain there until she was able to resume her training. But . . .

'Next Sunday do?'

'Sunday?'

He nodded. 'Then you can meet Aunt Norah, and settle in the flat. Be ready to start work for me on the Monday.'

Ah, yes, the flat. She must mention Simon. Or did it really matter? Perhaps he wouldn't notice . . .

'Now, about salary and hours,' he went on, and the opportunity for telling him passed. She would mention her nephew later. As late as possible, in case he changed his mind!

She was surprised at how much he was willing to pay. Surely it was above the going rate? But then, if his aunt was as hard to please as Mr Fielding, she would no doubt earn every penny.

The formalities concluded, he courteously

showed her out—into the pouring rain. It was a cold, showery afternoon, but she hadn't expected such heavy rain, nor was she prepared in any way. An umbrella and raincoat would have cluttered her up and wouldn't have looked good at an interview, but she had a plastic rain-hat attached to her key-ring, and she produced this now and proceeded to tuck every last reddish strand of hair inside.

Hallam watched, fascinated. 'It is pouring, Miss Weston. Surely that minute plastic thing isn't going to keep you dry?'

'It's all I have,' she said, simply. 'Don't worry,' she hurried on, misinterpreting his concerned glance, 'I won't get pneumonia and die before Sunday!'

She hurried out before he had time to comment.

Indeed, Pip was halfway down the long, winding drive before he could collect his wits and go after her. She had reached the wide, white entrance-gates before a peremptory 'toot' halted her in her tracks. It was the green sports-car.

Startled, she opened the gates as he obviously intended to go driving, gave him a cheery wave, despite the rain, and walked quickly down the lane to the bus-stop.

Raindrops were dripping from the front ridge of the rain-hat on to her nose and thence down her face, and several found their way to her un-protected neck, and she shivered.

How stupid not to have worn a mac! Then she remembered having lent it to Melanie, so she wasn't so stupid, after all. She had done her good deed, and they couldn't both wear the mac, could they?

The car caught up with her at the bus-stop. She

stood, a forlorn figure, keeping her back to the driving rain, and thinking deep, dark thoughts.

'If you had waited, Miss Weston,' a nasty voice spoke from the rolled-down window of the sports-car, 'I should have offered you a lift straight away.'

The door opened, and Pip thankfully snuggled herself in, dripping rain all over the surgeon's immaculate dark suit.

'You seem singularly lacking in common-sense,' he went on, and she tried to close her ears. He was a nagging old woman! She wondered if he was married, after all, but doubted that any woman could put up with him for very long. Divorced most likely, she decided.

She gave him Mrs Noakes's address, then realised he would know it, anyway, so she subsided quietly in the corner, and let him continue his nagging.

He pulled up outside Mrs Noakes's bungalow, and smiled at Pip.

Surprised but pleased, she smiled back, then beamed. Perhaps he might occasionally be pleasant! And what a difference when he smiled. He looked quite young.

'I hope you will be happy with us during your stay—be it short or long,' he murmured, still smiling gently.

'I'm sure I shall be. I'm looking . . . Oh!'

'Yes?'

'About the advert . . . I mean the advert said a child not objected to,' she ventured, deciding to be honest with him.

The smile died on his face, and he stared, blankly. 'Yes? What about it?'

'Well, there's Simon, you see,' she explained awkwardly. 'He's two and and there isn't anywhere else to take him.' There, it was out. Now she must tell him about her sister. He was entitled to some sort of explanation.

'I see.' The blank look slowly turned to one of shock, and the stormy eyes bored into hers again. 'A boy of two?'

'Mm. It's very difficult to explain—about Simon, I mean,' she wavered. 'You see, his father is . . .' but he cut her short.

'I do not want to hear about his father, Miss Weston!' he snarled, good humour entirely gone. 'His father is your concern, not mine! Naturally, if you have nowhere to leave the boy, you must bring him.'

Face set and angry, he reached across and opened the passenger-door for her. For an instant, his arm brushed accidentally against her breast, and she experienced again that feeling of mingled excitement and fear. She must be mad. He was old enough to be her father, and she didn't particularly like him, anyway!

Ashamed and disturbed by her feelings, she got out and turned to smile and say 'Thank-you', but the car shot off before she could utter a word.

It was just as she let herself into the side-door of the bungalow that she realised she'd said nothing about Melanie, and had only begun the few facts about Peter she was intending to divulge. She hadn't told him Simon was her nephew.

Surely he wouldn't think she had an illegitimate child—would he? Decisively, she shook her head. He wasn't stupid. He had only to re-read her references to see that she couldn't have taken the time off to have a baby. But Simon was born during the period she was out of work. She'd been nursing her mother. There were no references for *that* time.

Her cheeks were burning, despite the cold and the rain. He *did* think Simon was hers. His whole attitude changed once she mentioned Simon's father.

Unhappily, she pushed away the thought. On Sunday she would try to explain. Perhaps the autocratic Hallam Fielding might even smile at her again!

CHAPTER TWO

'Pip! It's lovely!' Melanie shared her sister's enthusiasm for the flat. She, too, went from room to room, exclaiming over the plain but good furniture, the fitted units in the kitchen, the pretty blue and white flowered curtains everywhere.

'It is cosy,' Pip agreed, as she and little Simon trailed along behind the slightly taller Melanie. 'And it's rent-free!'

'He could charge the earth for this place,' Melanie went on, as she gazed up at the only picture in the flat—a large, wood-framed print of 'The Haywain'. 'I wonder why he lets it free of charge?'

'To induce secretaries to stay once they've seen his Aunt Norah!' Pip laughed, but had never felt less like joking.

Simon, being at the 'terrible-twos' stage, went charging from room to room, shooting at imaginary monsters, and Pip shuddered. If anything should get damaged . . . She caught Melanie's gaze, and Simon reluctantly allowed himself to be picked up and cuddled.

'We have to be so careful, Melanie. It might be home for only a month.'

'Surely not?' Melanie turned blue eyes on her sister. Whereas Pip was on the plain side, Melanie was pretty—and knew it. 'I shall turn my charm on your horrid Mr Fielding,' she laughed.

Melanie was far too thin, Pip mused, but Mr Fielding might well find her attractive. If the formidable surgeon took a fancy to her, or to Simon, their troubles would be over. He would be bound to let Pip keep the job after her month's trial was up.

'Melanie,' she began, hesitantly, 'about Simon.'

'Yes?' Melanie broke off from swinging her son around.

'He, Mr Fielding, that is, thinks Simon is mine. I began to tell him about you but somehow he jumped to the conclusion that I am an unmarried mother,' Pip went on, miserably recalling his wrath.

'But that's perfect!'

Pip stared, open-mouthed, then began to protest.

'But it is!' Melanie insisted. 'If he thought Simon and I were free-loaders, he might not let us live here, but if he thinks *you* are Simon's mother and I'm just here to keep an eye on you both, he is bound to let us stay! Even after the month's trial. You'll be a wonderful secretary,' she hurried on. 'He won't get anyone else to work as hard as you!'

That was probably true, Pip agreed, silently. From the long list of duties Miss Tester, the surgeon's Aunt Norah, had reeled off, Pip doubted if she would even have time to draw breath between chores. Certainly Mr Fielding was getting his money's worth.

'If you don't tell him, just let him go on believing that you are Simon's mother, everything will work out fine!' Melanie said, airily.

'But I want him to know the truth!' Pip wailed. 'It's important that he believes me. I don't want him to think that . . . that I go around having love-children everywhere!'

Melanie giggled. 'Silly! It's only one love-child! It doesn't really matter, does it? He's fortyish, you said. You can't be falling for him, so what does his opinion matter?'

The bald truth was that it did matter. Pip wanted Mr Fielding to have a good opinion of her. She couldn't forget the contempt in his eyes when he'd misinterpreted her remarks about Simon and his father.

Aunt Norah had proved, on first acquaintance, to be every bit as crabby as she'd been warned.

Pip closed her eyes, trying to shut out the scene the day before. Melanie went whistling merrily out to the kitchen, and Simon trotted after her. Pip sat on the edge of the bed. With her eyes closed, she could almost see Hallam Fielding's face, the eyes full of loathing and anger, the thin mouth silent but condemning. She found herself wondering what it would be like to be kissed by such a man. What an odd thought!

Miss Tester was about seventy and a retired ward sister from a famous teaching hospital. She had made it clear that she did not approve of her nephew's choice of companion. Whilst her actual words were not insulting, her manner was, and Pip was left in no doubt about her status during the month's probation. The previous companion, Mrs Burr, had gone to live with her married daughter, but Miss Norah Tester hinted broadly that she could persuade the woman to return.

If Mrs Burr did return, she was gormless, Pip decided. No, Pip was lumbered, for the month at least. And if Mr Fielding took to Melanie and Simon the month would be extended, Aunt Norah or no Aunt Norah.

Pip had wondered, before meeting the woman, why the nephew should have to choose the companion rather than the old lady herself, but no longer wondered! No doubt Miss Tester put off prospective companions before they were even offered the job, and that was why she was landed with someone as young as Pip.

'Tea's ready!' Melanie called, and Pip composed her features. No point in depressing Melanie as well. She had problems enough.

'What will Peter do when he comes home?' Pip asked, over a simple tea of bread and jam and a rather stale currant cake. Melanie had slipped away earlier that day while her husband was at work. He knew of her decision to leave him, of course, but Melanie was afraid he would persuade her to change her mind, or even break down and cry, if he was at home when they left. The effect on Simon would be less, she judged, if they went while his Daddy was at work. Melanie hadn't told him where they were going, though. They would keep in touch through his sister, Gay.

Melanie lifted her shoulders in a depressed way. 'Get his tea, I suppose, just as we are. I left him a pie. He won't know we are here,' she added, giving Pip's hand a comforting squeeze. 'He won't find us in a month of Sundays.'

That was probably true. They were deep in the Surrey countryside, not more than twenty miles from Melanie and Peter's home but far off the beaten track. He would never expect to find them there, and Melanie intended to stay in. The baby would be able to play about in the yard.

And now, here they were. Over them hung the threat of dismissal for Pip before they were even settled, and then the problem of finding somewhere else.

Pip sighed, the burden of being in charge weighing heavily on her. The longed-for opportunity to resume her nursing career seemed further away than ever. So far away that she reckoned she would be too old by the time Melanie stopped leaning on her.

'Where is Mrs Mainwaring's letter?' Mr Fielding loomed over Pip as she sat at her electric typewriter two days later. Only two days and it seemed as if she'd been at his beck and call for years!

'Where is it supposed to be?' Pip asked sweetly, tossing back a lock of auburn hair.

'In my pending file, waiting to be answered,' Hallam Fielding said, quietly.

It was, she had found, an ominous sign when he spoke softly. The calm before the storm, as it were.

'Then it must be there,' Pip reasoned, not at all sure that it was. 'I'll look.'

'I have already looked, Miss Weston.'

'Oh!' She eyed him, doubtfully, then hastily stifled a yawn. Aunt Norah had insisted on watching the late film on TV and then demanded supper in bed afterwards, so naturally Pip had to return to the house to prepare it. Mrs Burr had, it seemed, always seen to Miss Tester's supper, and she expected Pip to add cooking to her long list of duties.

'If you find the work so tiring, Miss Weston,' he said, pointedly, 'perhaps you should try an occasional early night. The light was on in the flat at one o'clock this morning.'

'I know, but I'd only just . . .' but he waved her

explanation away.

She ran a hand distractedly through her long hair, which she was wearing loose, mainly because she hadn't expected her boss to be in. It hung in flowing curls almost to her shoulders. A gleaming sea of soft red-gold, and Mr Fielding seemed unable to take his eyes from it. Probably it annoyed him.

No, Mrs Mainwaring's letter wasn't in his pending. 'I know,' Pip said, brightly. 'I filed it under M.' She hurried to the filing cabinet, pulled open the third drawer and rustled through the M miscellaneous. Not there. It must be in Mrs Mainwaring's notes. She had put the notes to one side as the patient was being seen later that afternoon.

'Here we are!' Triumphantly, she held the letter aloft. 'I *thought* I had filed it.'

Hallam almost snatched it from her. Shrugging, she opened her desk drawer and selected a thick rubber band. That would keep her hair out of the way. There, that looked more business-like.

But it did nothing to stem the surgeon's anger. 'What did you do that for?'

'It seemed to be annoying you!' she said, petulantly. 'You keep staring at my hair, so . . .'

A thin smile crossed his face, briefly. 'I was thinking your hair reminded me of my brother's. He's a real carrot-top!'

'Is he? I didn't know you had any relatives,' she began, then her pale skin burned as she realised what she'd so nearly said.

He read her mind accurately, and she blushed more. 'You mean as I was spawned by the Devil I couldn't possibly have a brother? Or parents, either, I suppose?' he went on, drily.

'Well . . . You *do* have an Aunt,' she said, uncomfortably.

'But *what* an Aunt! Giving you a hard time, is she?'

She hedged, but those cold eyes held her prisoner, and she couldn't lie, so contented herself with a nod.

'I warned you she was crabby. Anyhow, my brother Geoffrey is coming down shortly. He's a GP in the heart of Yorkshire. You can see his hair for yourself.'

'Did he get called Carrot-top at school?' she asked, pleased because he seemed to have forgotten he was cross with her.

'Carrots, usually, I believe. Don't tell me you were called that?' He ran disbelieving eyes over the lovely red-gold hair.

'Mm. Sometimes Ginger. I hate my hair!' she said vehemently. She didn't really, but she had certainly hated being ginger as a child. Hated being thin and plain, as well. What fun the boys at school had teasing her, making her life a misery. Yet she'd never cried, thus denying them the ultimate pleasure. No-one ever knew how much she'd suffered.

'Hate it?' Hallam Fielding said, wonderingly, putting out a hand towards her hair, then just as swiftly withdrawing it again. 'It's a beautiful colour, Miss Weston. A greaty many brunettes try to achieve such a colour with the aid of artificial tints, but there is nothing like a genuine redhead!'

Pleased, she beamed, quite forgetting that he didn't like her, and, indeed, seemed to like her even less when she smiled.

Much less when she smiled, because the frosty

expression was back again and, imperiously, he waved the mislaid letter at her. 'Next time you file one of my letters,' he fumed, 'make sure it has been answered first!'

Pip sighed. 'I'm very sorry. Truly I am,' she assured him, sounding so mournful that the surgeon shot her a concerned glance.

'Is the job getting on top of you already?'

Pip, quick to sense his disappointment in her, assured him it wasn't. 'It's interesting!' she insisted. 'When I eventually go back to general, I shall know about all sorts of conditions I didn't know before!'

Hallam smiled distantly, secretly pleased at her enthusiasm. It was years since he'd been young and enthusiastic, perhaps he never was. He frowned, trying to remember his days as a medical student.

Pip misinterpreted the frown. He was cross with her again! It wasn't fair. If she smiled at him, that was wrong. If she yawned, the job was more than she could cope with. If she mis-filed something, he held a Post-Mortem on the minor misdemeanour. He was impossible! Simply impossible! He . . .

'Tell me about Mrs Mainwaring's condition,' the subject of her dark thoughts said, suddenly.

Disconcerted, Pip was silent for a moment, trying to recollect her thoughts. 'Oh, yes. She has carcinoma of the breast and you're operating tomorrow.'

'How did you come to diagnose carcinoma, Miss Weston?' the surgeon enquired, mildly.

'Um, she complained of a lump in her breast.'

'Well? Go on.'

'Um, her GP examined her and made a provisional diagnosis of carcinoma,' Pip went on, uncertainly.

'*Why* was it provisional, Miss Weston?'

'He wasn't sure. With some lumps it's possible to say they are either malignant or not, but with others a definite diagnosis isn't possible,' Pip hurried on, pleased she had remembered.

'So? If a differential diagnosis is made, the lump *could* be non-cancerous, then?' Hallam asked, suavely, and Pip nodded.

'Therefore,' he continued, making her feel gauche and very stupid, 'we cannot be sure until an exploratory operation has been carried out. *You* cannot say that she has carcinoma of the breast, can you?'

'No,' Pip agreed. 'A lump isn't always malignant.'

'A lump is usually benign, Miss Weston. We must expect the worst but hope for the best. Mrs Mainwaring, judging from her history and symptoms and going by my experience, probably *does* have carcinoma, but you do see the danger of jumping to conclusions, don't you?'

Pip's mouth tightened. He was a fine one to talk about jumping to conclusions! Hadn't he assumed that Simon was hers? *And* without a shred of evidence!

She contented herself with nodding agreement, though. Anything for a quiet life.

He sighed, heavily, then the door closed noisily behind him. He never actually *banged* doors, but was patently unable to close them quietly.

They had a further confrontation that evening at the flat. Pip's duties for Aunt Norah had finished at seven o'clock. For once, the old lady had decided on an early night with a good book.

Pip also wanted to read a good book—one of the text-books Mr Fielding had promised her she might read. Not wanting to cross his path again that afternoon, she had sneaked the book out of the cupboard without asking him. It never occurred to her that he might want to refer to it, though it was a medical rather than a nursing textbook.

Pip was washing-up after the evening meal, while Mel read a story to Simon, when the door of the flat opened and Hallam Fielding appeared.

'I did knock but no-one was listening,' he began, nastily, then saw Melanie. Her honey-blonde hair was loose, and clung prettily because it was not quite dry. Pip had at last persuaded her sister to take an interest in herself.

Pip held her breath as her handsome employer and her beautiful sister eyed each other.

Something went thud inside Pip. It was important that Hallam Fielding took to Melanie. But, then, how could he resist her? Of course, he could not.

Slowly, Melanie got to her feet, leaving an almost-asleep Simon on the narrow bed. She held out a hand which the surgeon took—and held on to.

Neither of them heard poor Pip's sharp intake of breath. There was a tight feeling across her chest. Heartburn, most likely. She licked suddenly dry lips. 'This ... this is my sister, Melanie, Mr Fielding. This is Hallam Fielding, Melanie. My employer.'

Reluctantly, it seemed, Mr Fielding released Melanie's hand and smiled at her. Actually smiled! Pip couldn't believe it. All she ever got were scowls, sharp comments, harsh words ...

'I don't seem to recall you mentioning a sister, Miss Weston,' Hallam Fielding said, smoothly, his eyes hooded as he turn to Pip. The aquiline nostrils were flaring, and she knew he was fighting for control. He wanted to tear her apart verbally but wouldn't be discourteous in front of Melanie.

Pip studied Simon's sleeping form, and a tender smile touched her mouth. Poor little soul. She tried to draw inspiration from him, but nothing came. When she bravely met Mr Fielding's storm-grey eyes again she wished she had not. Anger and contempt were there for all to see, and Pip couldn't possibly have misinterpreted the look. It was pure hate.

She swallowed, nervously. Surely she hadn't committed such a crime? He didn't need the flat. What did it matter if there were two women there instead of one? It wasn't enough to inspire such dislike.

Impetuously, Melanie laid her hand on the surgeon's arm, and smiled shyly. And, gently, he smiled down at her.

'Please, sir, Mr Fielding. I have something to explain—about us, I mean,' Melanie rushed on, her breathless little-girl voice irresistible. At least, Pip thought it was. 'Pip realises you have a right to an explanation.' Here she flashed a smile at Pip. 'But if you could spare me a few minutes?' she asked, blue eyes eloquent in their appeal.

Hallam Fielding did not, Pip noted, try to dislodge Melanie's clinging hand. With Melanie still attempting to explain, they moved out to the sitting-room, leaving Pip in the bedroom with the boy.

She sank heavily on to Melanie's bed. They had

managed to get the two beds into the bigger room, while Pip spent her nights in a sleeping bag in front of the settee.

Melanie's charm would wear him down. Pip knew she ought to be pleased. Melanie was trying so hard for both of them, for them all. She would be telling him about the mistake, explaining that Simon was *her* son, not Pip's. He would feel sorry for them and let them all stay until Melanie's private life was sorted out. Once he knew who Simon's mother was, Pip was sure he would look more kindly on her again.

She lay back on the bed and clasped her hands behind her head, feeling more relaxed. Melanie would make him understand.

'I came for my textbook, Miss Weston.' Hallam Fielding's crisp tones woke Pip, and she sat up suddenly.

Heavens, she must have dozed! Melanie stood by his side, and winked at her sister as if to reassure her that everything was settled. Relieved, Pip smiled at them both, and scrambled up, hastily. So hastily that she banged her knee on the corner of the bed. Discomfited, she risked a glance at the surgeon. Dark grey eyes stared back. No, he certainly was *not* in a good mood. Melanie's wink had been too optimistic.

Feeling foolish, Pip assured Mr Fielding that his book was quite safe, that she was sorry for borrowing it without permission.

A disbelieving snort was the only reply she got, and she stood on one of the chairs to retrieve the book which she'd placed on top of the wardrobe out of Simon's way.

It was heavy, and the chair wobbled danger-ously. If I break a leg now, he'll be delighted, she thought, unhappily. He will be able to lecture me on my carelessness.

She turned to hand him the book, but found herself taking off into space, book and all, as the surgeon swung her down. Briefly, his capable hands were about her slender waist, and she enjoyed the contact which, alas, was over too soon.

Feeling dizzy, she gave him the book with a murmur of thanks. A curt nod and an equally curt 'Goodnight' was all she got in reply, as the door closed behind him.

She was cold. The warmth of his hands left her wanting more. She had wanted him to go on holding her! 'Well, *did* you charm him?' she asked her sister, over-brightly.

Melanie's eyes danced. 'I'm sure of it! He said of course I must stay to keep an eye on you both. He said you were obviously incapable of managing by yourself, but that you were a good worker and he didn't want to let you go prematurely!'

Pip opened her mouth to speak but couldn't find words. 'What was that about you keeping an eye on me?' she managed, at last. 'You told him about Simon, didn't you?' she went on, suspiciously, only to have her worst fears confirmed when her sister shook her head.

'How could I, Pip? I thought we'd agreed that Simon was to be passed off as yours? Anyway,' Melanie went on, defensively, 'he didn't give me a chance to explain. He kept going on about you and saying how you needed putting on the right road, and . . .'

'What!' Pip shrieked, then, remembering Simon,

lowered her voice. 'I *am* on the right road!' she whispered, fiercely. 'You are the one who wants putting right. Mr Fielding ought to be shaking some sense into *you*, not me!'

Without waiting for any weak protestations from her sister, Pip flung herself out of the flat, and hurried down the steps. Without knowing how she got there, not even aware that she was going in that direction, she found herself outside Hallam Fielding's study window.

He was at his desk, with his back to the window, head bent over a book, presumably the one she had borrowed without permission. The velvet curtains were drawn back and she could gaze her fill, knowing that he was unlikely to turn around.

A deep sadness filled her and she couldn't understand why. She felt homesick, yet for what or where? She didn't know. What she did know was that she wanted to put her arms around Hallam's neck and press her cheek to his, and run loving fingers through that crisp, slightly greying hair.

Horrified by her thoughts, she walked disconsolately away. She had problems enough without adding a stupid infatuation to them.

CHAPTER THREE

'MR FIELDING sees private patients only in the afternoons,' Sister Farrell said briskly, and Pip nodded.

'Every afternoon?'

Sister Farrell pursed her lips in that disapproving way of hers, and Pip felt about an inch tall. 'Of course not! Do you not think the wee man deserves a day off?' Jessica Farrell, a retired hospital Sister and Hallam Fielding's part-time nurse, was horrified. 'He gives consultations three afternoons a week.'

She hesitated, then her tall, starchy person unbent a little at the misery in Pip's eyes. 'Are you *sure* you can manage, Miss Weston? We could get someone from the agency, if it is too . . .'

'Oh, no! Please. I did some of my general training,' Pip pointed out, but her words did nothing to reassure the older woman.

'Yes, so I hear, but you left without giving nursing a chance, didn't you? And,' she went on, relentlessly, as Pip was about to interrupt, 'it's no use making the excuse that you were nursing your mother during her terminal carcinoma. I understand that, but surely you could have re-commenced training by now?'

Pip sighed. She was about to re-start her training when Melanie's marital troubles had bubbled up again. She had actually written several letters of application. Oh, how she longed to get back into uniform! Even the dubious delights of cleaning the sluice, or doing endless bedpan rounds would be welcome. For that reason, she must make a success of the ten days she was to spend as Sister Farrell's holiday relief.

There would be no actual bedside nursing, naturally. All she had to do was act as chaperone when Mr Fielding was examining female patients, assist them to undress, keep appointments, make sure the consultant had his notes, etc, for lectures or operating sessions. It all seemed perfectly straightforward, and she was eagerly looking forward to meeting the first patient.

She might not be the world's best filing clerk, but nursing was something she had taken to like a duck to water, and she intended to make herself so indispensable to Hallam Fielding that he would beg her to stay at the end of her month's trial.

Pip had part of two afternoons with Sister Farrell, learning what was expected of her. In addition, she still had to type the surgeon's letters, do the general office work, *and* cope with Aunt Norah. Miss Norah Tester was one person's work in herself!

After Pip had shown the last patient out on the second afternoon, she had her first argument with Miss Tester. Jessica Farrell and Hallam Fielding were closeted in his office, discussing weighty medical matters, and Pip had just returned to her typewriter when Miss Tester stormed in, her lined face even greyer than usual.

'I have been waiting for the best part of an hour, young woman! I do not enjoy good health,' she panted, 'yet I have to come to seek *you*,' Miss Tester went on. 'You are supposed to be my com-

panion. You ought to be within calling distance!'
Miss Tester's voice rose an octave, and Pip hurriedly found her a chair, aware that the fit of
temper might well bring on the woman's angina.

'I'm sorry you looked for me and I wasn't there,'
she said, placatingly. 'Mr Fielding had a clinic this
afternoon and I've been helping,' she pointed out.
'I have to learn the ropes as . . .'

Miss Tester stopped her with an imperious wave.
'My needs come first. You were supposed to sit
with me while I watched the television serial. I *told*
you!'

Pip nibbled her lower lip, aware that Miss Tester
was right. Yet how could she be in two or more
places at once? She was no better than a skivvy!

'I had to be here to learn from Sister Farrell,'
Pip said, shakily, trying to keep her temper. What
use was a quick-tempered nurse? 'I'm very sorry,
Miss Tester, but you could have managed to watch
TV without me. Mr Fielding needs me here,
and . . .'

'Mr Fielding never needed you!' his aunt
stormed. 'You are useless! Worse than useless! And
you with an . . . a child,' she finished, obviously
not able to use the word 'illegitimate'. 'He has said
as much.'

'He's said what?' Pip asked, then wished she
hadn't, as Miss Tester flashed her a triumphant
look.

'He said you . . .'

'That you are a hard-working young lady and
he is glad of your help,' a harsh voice broke in,
and both women turned. Pip's big eyes held tears
she couldn't hide, but couldn't let fall, and hastily,
she turned away and began to rifle aimlessly

through the filing cabinet.

Hallam Fielding stalked into the room, and although Pip's back was turned, she knew he was glaring at both her and his Aunt Norah. Their silly argument had interrupted his session with Sister Farrell.

'Shall I give you an arm, Aunt Norah?' the surgeon asked, tightly, and Pip swung round. Miss Tester's face was pinched and blue again, and she appeared to be in pain.

Immediately, Pip went to the old woman's side but, irritably, Hallam Fielding waved her away. 'Sister and I will manage!'

Rebuffed, she went back to the typewriter while the other two soothed Miss Tester. She had tablets which had to be dissolved sublingually, to ease the heart pains, but Pip didn't hear her nephew suggest she take one. Perhaps he knew it was a childish tantrum on Miss Tester's part.

They were helping her to her feet, and she was clinging piteously to Hallam, when a new, cheerful voice broke in: 'Hullo! Auntie having another attack? Who has thwarted you this time, Auntie?'

A younger, broader version of Hallam Fielding walked in, and Pip's eyes widened. Yes, he was a redhead all right, though his thick, straight hair was a much darker red than hers. She perked up immediately. For no reason at all, she felt she'd found an ally.

Aunt Norah visibly softened. What might have been a smile came to her severe face and she held out her arms to the newcomer.

Hallam watched in silence. There was a sardonic twist to his mouth, and Pip felt for him. Evidently brother Geoff was favourite.

Realising she was staring, Pip flushed. She was paid to work. Heaven only knew how she was going to get through all the notes she had to type. The sooner she started, the better. Ignoring the scene of welcome, she switched on the typewriter, and the slight noise focussed Geoffrey Fielding's attention on her.

'A redhead! Brother Hallam, you show good taste!' he chuckled, holding out his hand to Pip who, hesitantly, rose and summoned a polite smile. Her vibrant hair was in a demure bun and looked darker than it actually was.

Sorrowfully, Dr Fielding shook his head. 'This won't do at all, Nurse. We redheads must expose our hair to the elements!'

Pip's hand strayed defensively to her bun as she backed away, causing Dr Fielding more merriment. He was about to make some ribald comment, she felt sure, but Hallam came to her rescue. Taking his brother firmly by the arm, and with Sister Farrell and Aunt Norah following, he led them from the room. The door closed softly behind them, and Pip let out her breath in a long sigh.

However would she cope? This emotional hangup over Hallam Fielding was bad enough and was beginning to cause her sleepless nights, but to be drawn into a heated argument with his Aunt, then having the brother teasing her—it was all too much.

She sank down in the small easy chair by the window, put her head down, and just cried. Not loudly, not a wild wailing, just tears of great sadness. One after the other they ran down her cheeks, along the bridge of her straight little nose, and splashed on to her clenched hands. She hated them all! It was stupid, illogical and very, very childish, but she did, she did! And there was nowhere for her to turn, no-one with whom to share her sorrow. She was almost alone in the world except for Melanie. And it was no use crying on *her* shoulder.

Just once, it would have been nice to open her tired heart, pour out all her troubles, be soothed and reassured. Instead, at twenty, she might as well have been a lonely old maid already. Nobody cared!

She allowed herself to wallow in self-pity for several minutes. She recognised it for what it was but couldn't stem the flow of tears. Eventually, though, they stopped and, with eyes red and swollen and a blotchy face, she went towards her desk, only to find Geoffrey Fielding standing beside the door, which she knew had been securely closed.

Defiantly, she met his concerned gaze. Just let him tease her, she was more than ready for him!

'I'm sorry, little Miss Weston,' Geoffrey said gently, coming into the office and closing the door. 'Did my teasing upset you that much?'

Mutely, she shook her head, then, restlessly, began to sort papers on her too-small desk.

'You must have been teased at school about being a carrot-top,' he went on, perching on the end of the desk. 'Hallam took me to task. Put me right in my place!' he chuckled, and she gave him a shy smile. Perhaps he wasn't so bad, after all.

'We redheads must stick together!' she managed to quip, and he beamed.

'That's more like it! Hallam says I must be kind to you and not upset you with any unforeseen moves! He tells me you've had a hard life and need looking after,' he went on.

Gravely, she said: 'Did he tell you I am a fallen angel?'

Geoffrey Fielding hesitated. 'That, too,' he finally admitted.

'I hate your brother!' Pip's words shocked herself even more than they did Geoffrey. 'He's so . . . so smug! And self-righteous! How dare he call me names! He doesn't know half the story,' she hurried on, staring down at the typewriter. If Hallam had walked in at that moment, she might well have thrown the heavy machine at him.

'What he doesn't know, he has pieced together, young lady,' Geoffrey said gently, resting a kindly hand on her shoulder. 'He is as concerned about your welfare as your sister is. He says she has come to stay here to give you a hand with the child, so at least one person thinks you are worthy.'

His hand moved gently over her slender shoulders, and with his thumb he caressed the nape of her neck.

Pip found herself relaxing, beginning to unwind, just a little. His touch was kindly, nothing more, and she allowed it to continue. Then the image of Hallam Fielding intruded as it did so often, and she jerked away.

'I have to get on,' she said a trifle breathlessly. 'Mr Fielding expects his reports before he goes to the conference tomorrow. I haven't even started them yet!' The sound she made was a choked-off sob, but she hoped he would mistake it for a laugh.

'You start the reports and I'll bring you a nice, frosty glass of orange-juice! I could do with one,' he said, making for the door and giving her no chance to protest.

Methodically, she sorted the sheets of foolscap paper all covered with her employer's small, neat handwriting. For a doctor his writing was surprisingly legible, and she knew the task shouldn't take more than two hours. Provided she could concentrate, she mused wryly. Concentration was becoming surprisingly difficult these days. She loathed Hallam Fielding! And his crabby old Aunt Norah! Another tear forced itself out but she refused to stop what she was doing.

Still crying quietly, she arranged the paper and carbon, and prepared to type. The machine wasn't simply a smarter version of a manual typewriter. It was far more complicated and her fingers rarely seemed to hit the right keys. She would far rather nurse than do office-work but we can't always have what we want, she mused, hastily wiping her face with the back of her hand. The tears were obstructing her vision, and she must type his notes nicely. He *must* be pleased with her!

A large, spotless white handkerchief was dangled over her left shoulder, and she took it without pausing to look up. 'Thank you, Dr Fielding,' she muttered, mopping up the tears.

'*Mr* Fielding,' a voice said calmly, and she whirled round.

'Oh! I'm sorry, sir. I'm just typing your report for tomorrow,' she said, unnecessarily.

'So I see. Why are you crying, Miss Weston?' Hallam Fielding sounded resigned, and Pip tensed, mentally preparing for a fight.

He pulled up a chair close to the desk and sat down, very, very near to poor Pip, and she tried desperately to find the right keys. Shutting her eyes tightly, she found the home keys on the typewriter,

but before she could begin, her hands were
engulfed in his, and squeezed, gently.

The sensation was pleasant, far too pleasant, and
Pip tried to prise her hands free of his grip, but
without success.

'Must I always repeat myself, Miss Weston?' He
didn't sound resigned now, he sounded angry, in a
clinical sort of way, and Pip licked her suddenly
dry lips.

'I'm feeling a bit under the weather, but I'll be
OK in a minute,' she assured him, managing to
meet the cold eyes.

'If ever you need a fatherly figure to confide in,
Miss Weston,' he said, unexpectedly, 'please feel
free to use me as a substitute father. Or uncle, if
you prefer,' he added, wryly.

Startled, she began to shake her head. He wasn't
at all avuncular, and most certainly *not* fatherly!

Geoffrey Fielding came upon them then as they
sat, Pip's small hands in his brother's, the two exchanging earnest glances.

The orange-juice spilled over, and he muttered
a swear-word, causing Pip to go bright red. Not
because of the swearing but for what Dr Fielding
had seen, or *thought* he had seen.

The reality, unfortunately, was very different!
Being offered a fatherly shoulder to cry on by a
man you found attractive and almost irresistible,
wasn't Pip's idea of heaven.

To her surprise, her boss hurriedly removed his
hand. In amazement, she watched the swift flow of
colour over his lean face, as the brothers stared at
each other.

Pip swallowed. They looked, to her over-active
imagination, like two cockerels squaring up for a

fight. She had the crazy feeling that she was the hen in the middle!

'I brought your drink,' Geoffrey said, his tone aggrieved, and she gave him a warm smile. His kindness touched her, when all around she saw enemies. He might prove to be an ally when, as seemed inevitable, his brother gave her notice at the end of her month's trial.

Her employer gave what sounded like a snort and strode out, the door closing noisily as usual.

'I'm afraid I have offended Mr Fielding,' Pip said nervously, as, in his turn, Geoffrey sat beside her, a broader version of Hallam, but with eyes a lighter, almost blue-grey.

'Offended wasn't the term I would use,' he said quietly. 'He seemed quite taken with you. Sorry I interrupted!'

'No, no!' Pip said, exasperated. Her temper was fast rising, and she wanted to shake him, shake both of them. 'He found me crying and offered me a hankie,' she explained, producing the hankie which she had tucked into the pocket of her gaily-printed skirt. 'He offered me a shoulder to cry on,' she said, then realised how unwise she'd been when Geoffrey Fielding's eyebrows shot up.

'*Did* he? You want to be careful. Older men have a weakness for sweet young redheads!'

He seemed to be only half-joking, and again, Pip wanted to shake him. 'Mr Fielding isn't *that* old!' she retorted. 'He has been kind to me—to us all, and I'm grateful.'

Ignoring him, she took a long drink of the delicious fruit juice, then began at last to type. It would be well into the evening before she finished even if she didn't stop for tea. She would hurry to the flat when she was halfway through, grab a few sandwiches, and eat them while she worked.

Busy with her thoughts, she didn't see Dr Fielding leave, very quietly in contrast to the surgeon.

'Isn't it exciting, Pip! An evening out!' Melanie was bubbling over, and Pip, who couldn't share her enthusiasm, felt she was being a wet blanket as she said worriedly: 'Are you sure it's wise? Someone might see you.'

It was a lame remark, and Melanie stared at her, eyes wary. 'No-one will recognise me, silly! We're too far away from home.' A sad expression crossed her pretty face, and Pip assumed she was thinking of the home she'd left. True, it was only a council house but half the furniture was Melanie's. She and her husband had bought it lovingly, item by item.

It must be very hard to leave a home, Pip thought. But never having had a home, she couldn't feel for her sister *that* much. Their parents had split up soon after Melanie's birth and both were now dead. Pip had gone back to nurse her mother, but it hadn't seemed like a home.

Would Melanie start divorce proceedings? Pip wondered, or would the trial separation make her realise how much she missed Peter?

Suppose she fancies Hallam? a little voice whispered in Pip's ear. Then she seemed to hear it laugh, maliciously. Of course Melanie wouldn't be interested in Hallam. She'd said she still loved her husband. Hallam was far too old for her . . . yet he *had* invited her out for the evening.

'Don't worry about Simon,' Pip said, gazing at the top of his blond head. 'I'll see he goes to bed at the usual time. Miss Tester has taken off to visit friends, so she won't want my company this evening.'

That, at least, was a relief. Miss Tester was becoming crabbier, if that was possible. Though she clearly adored her nephew, Geoffrey, having him in the house did not improve her temper or her manners. Still she made no attempt to hide her dislike of Pip. She, in turn, was finding it harder and harder to hold on to her temper, and tried to meet abuse with politeness, scorn with a dignified silence, but it was by no means easy.

It was three days since Dr Fielding's arrival, and he showed no signs of hurrying back to his practice. His manner towards Pip was polite but no longer friendly. Possibly he believed she was after his brother. Hallam was, as usual, polite and distant, and did not repeat his offer of a shoulder to cry on, even when he came upon her that morning with her face still tear-streaked because of some catty remark of his Aunt's.

The evening stretched ahead, and promised to be a long and lonely one. Once she had seen Melanie off, Pip took Simon around the lovely, scented flower-garden before bed.

Melanie looked stunning, wearing Pip's only good dress, a soft brown Indian cotton patterned in black and gold. It went so well with her honey-blonde hair. Much better than with Pip's red mop, she had to admit. Melanie wore her own gold clover-leaf earrings and Pip's pretty gold and silver bangles.

Hallam didn't call for her, so Pip was spared that much, but her heart lurched as her sister went tripping gaily down the steps, and Pip's mournful gaze followed her across the courtyard, and she continued to watch long after the rear-door to the house had closed.

Restlessly, she patrolled the gardens with Simon, even after he had fallen asleep, his fair head cradled against her shoulder. He asked once or twice where his Mummy was, but didn't appear all that concerned; unlike his Auntie Pip who was very concerned indeed!

The garden was endless. There was a rock-garden just beyond the garage and courtyard, then came the roses, which Pip had admired on her first day. She had a good view of them from the kitchen window.

Then came acres of lawn. At least, the lawns seemed to go on for acres. To the right were a few plum trees, then a wide area where, Sister Farrell told her, Mr Fielding had kept a donkey until recently. Now there was a chicken-run, and lots of derelict buildings, with, occasionally, an oasis of flowers or flowering weeds. A perfect play-ground for children, Pip thought, as she headed towards it.

She couldn't imagine the austere surgeon keeping a donkey. It was completely out of character. Apparently, he'd bought it from an itinerant, who had starved it until its bones were visible. Although it had the best of care afterwards, Hallam's kindly gesture had been too late. The donkey had been old, in any case.

Pip felt sad when she heard the story. Her warm heart had room enough for all suffering creatures, animal as well as human. The episode proved Mr Fielding wasn't as unfeeling as he liked to make out, and Pip's heart warmed to him. Though if he took her sister out often, she wasn't going to think *that* highly of him!

She was deep in her anatomy and physiology book when she heard the big car come to a purring halt. Eleven-thirty. Pip was tired and longed to go to bed, but she had to admit Melanie wasn't all that late. It would do her sister good, anyway.

She listened for Melanie's light step coming up, but was horrified when she heard *two* lots of footsteps. She was bringing him in for coffee!

Almost falling over her feet in her haste, Pip rushed out to the kitchen to put the kettle on. She was busily arranging cups and saucers on a tray when Melanie called out that she had brought a guest back with her.

Reluctantly, Pip went to meet them. Her sister looked radiant. There was at last some colour in her cheeks. Her hair, newly curled by Pip, shone with health, her lovely eyes sparkled, and whatever the evening had done to Pip, it had certainly done a great deal for her sister.

Hallam Fielding was immaculate in dinner-jacket, greying hair brushed straight back, but as unsmiling as ever. That, at least, was a relief to poor Pip. If he'd come in grinning from ear to ear, she could not have coped.

'C . . . coffee's on its way,' she managed, avoiding her employer's quizzical gaze.

'Lovely, Pip. Thank you for all the trouble you've taken.' Melanie's tinkling laugh grated on Pip's nerves, and she wished she would stop, then knew it was unfair. It was good to hear Melanie laugh again.

'Hallam admired your dress, Pip. It's so lovely and soft.' Melanie twirled around in front of them, and Pip's heart dropped to her comfortable old bedroom slippers. It was Hallam now, was it?

When side by side with her glamorous sister, Pip knew how she looked. A plain, if pleasant face, an ordinary little nose and hair the colour of uncooked carrots. Hardly enticing!

Just then Simon woke. Seeing his mother, he held out his arms. 'Mummy! Mummy come!'

Melanie hurried across and cradled her son against her chest, while Pip went first white with shock, then red as the surgeon's dark, accusing gaze held hers.

Well, it was better this way, she thought, defensively. Unconsciously, she squared her shoulders, daring him to make trouble. They ought to have told him before that Simon was Melanie's child. It didn't matter now that he knew. He was clearly smitten with Melanie so wasn't likely to turn them out.

He looked anything but smitten as he muttered 'Goodnight, ladies,' and left without waiting for coffee, leaving Pip anxious and ill-at-ease. Perhaps he thought Melanie was the unmarried mother now.

The kettle whistled, and she hurried out to prepare the coffee. Melanie appeared to have noticed nothing amiss, and, indeed, was so used to being called 'Mummy' that it probably hadn't occurred to her that the knowledge would come as a great shock to Hallam Fielding.

Could it be that he had fallen for Melanie? The awful thought wouldn't go away. Although Pip was glad her reputation was no longer sullied, she felt sympathy for Hallam, finding out so abruptly that the woman he cared for had a small child and, possibly, a husband.

Mr Fielding's clinic was particularly busy next day. Whatever else she might say about him, Pip couldn't fault his keenness. Of course, she could be cynical and say that he took such an interest in his private patients because they paid him well. But that would be unfair, for she felt sure he took an equally caring interest in his National Health patients. She didn't know; it was just a feeling she had about him. He was a *caring* person.

Pip was sorry her time with the patients was to be only a short one. She would cheerfully have taken over Sister Farrell's job—thankfully leaving the tall Scotswoman to cope with Aunt Norah!

They had coped with a variety of medical problems this afternooon, Pip mused as she helped Mrs Abbott to get dressed. There was Mrs Douch with suspected cholccystitis. She had taken up more of Mr Fielding's time than Pip had allowed for. The consultant wasn't satisfied about the woman, Pip knew. In addition, she was getting on in years and Pip wondered how she would stand up to the strain of an operation. Then Lady Kathleen turned up, nearly twenty minutes early for her appointment and demanding to be seen straight away. After that there had been two ladies presenting with unexplained lumps. She was glad there was nothing terribly wrong with Mrs Abbott, who was a cheerful soul.

'You're so helpful, Nurse. It's these corsets, see.' Mrs Abbott talked on, but Pip didn't hear more than one word in three.

Hallam Fielding hadn't spoken to her since last night. His conversation was largely confined to a series of ill-humoured grunts, and Pip couldn't take much more. If he was angry, and his dark, intense face certainly gave every sign of it, why couldn't he shout at her, throw a book? Anything would be better than the brooding silence. He made use of gestures whenever possible, and Pip was busy fighting the urge to gesture back, a very rude gesture, too!

Sighing, she smiled reassuringly at little Mrs Abbott. Pip had been relieved to read on her card that only 'Tender Loving Care' was needed. For her age, Mrs Abbott appeared in good shape, except for being about a stone overweight, and she and Pip had a struggle to lace up her heavy surgical corsets.

'Such a nice doctor. He's got lovely eyes,' Mrs Abbot enthused. 'Such long lashes for a man, too!'

Pip smiled to herself. They *were* long lashes, but did nothing to warm the cold restless eyes they protected. A block of ice. That's what he was. Cold and empty, Pip said, inwardly. She really could not stand the man.

Having seen a happy Mrs Abbott off the premises, Pip began to tidy up.

There was a fresh sheet and blanket for the examination couch, the desk to be tidied, various instruments to be put away.

Nearly being a nurse but not quite, she mused, as she lovingly ran her fingers along the stethoscope.

'It is not a toy to play with, Miss Weston!' A thunderous-browed Hallam Fielding loomed over her, and in her fright she dropped the instrument. Both bent down to retrieve it, and he lowered his head until his angry eyes were on a level with her own.

'Why did you lie about the child!' he snapped, and she gasped at the unfairness.

'I did *not* lie!' she snapped back. 'You assumed from the first that Simon was mine and didn't give me a chance to explain!'

'Nonsense! You are a devious little madam! Letting me feel sorry for you, wanting to protect you from yourself!'

'Did you really want to protect me?' If he did, then he must like her a little, surely?

'I'm not sure which of us needs protecting, Miss Weston,' he said, bleakly. Then he gathered the instruments together, closed the cupboard and walked back to his office.

CHAPTER FOUR

'DON'T tell me *you* are little Miss Weston?'

Pip and the elegant brunette stared at each other, both surprised. In Pip's case it amounted to shock, for Vanessa Clifton had introduced herself as Hallam Fielding's fiancée.

'Why shouldn't I be?' Pip faltered, wrinkling her nose a little as the tiny brunette gently pushed by, leaving behind a cloud of what Pip recognised as Panache perfume.

It was a scent she liked but felt it too sophisticated for plain Pip Weston. She sniffed it in avidly as she followed Miss Clifton to the waiting-room.

'I shall wait here for my darling,' Miss Clifton said, sweetly. 'He doesn't like people wandering over his private apartments—even me,' she said, shooting Pip another surprised glance. 'I thought Hallam was teasing me,' she went on, her green eyes sweeping over Pip from the top of her neatly plaited and coiled hair to the toes of her comfortable sandals. 'He said . . .' But she couldn't go on, and Pip had to stand uncomfortably by as the older girl went into trills of laughter.

She was beautiful, Pip thought resentfully, but her personality wasn't as attractive as Melanie's. How could he possibly prefer Vanessa Clifton? And to get engaged to her!

He was playing fast and loose with her sister's affections. He had taken her out on three occasions since last week and he had no right, no right at all!

The brunette dabbed carefully at her eyes with a wisp of lacy handkerchief, Pip, who used practical Kleenex, noted disparagingly.

'I *am* sorry,' Miss Clifton continued, 'but if you could hear what Hallam says about you! I imagined he was joking, and I came here today with talons at the ready!' She was almost overcome by her mirth again, and Pip stared fascinated, as she waved a maroon-fingernailed hand at her. 'I saw dear Geoff in the front garden with a strange girl this morning, but I didn't realise it was you. I have come to do battle for my dearest, thinking you must be some tall, sophisticated redhead!'

'Well, I'm not, am I?' Pip retorted. 'Exactly what *did* Mr Fielding say about me?' It was playing into the woman's hands, but Pip simply had to know.

'He said you were a sweet little carrot-topped girl and I must be nice to you!' Miss Clifton laughed.

Pip closed her eyes in pain, but said nothing. She could well imagine Mr Fielding saying such a thing.

'You *are* carrotty, aren't you?' Miss Clifton rose, gracefully, and moved nearer to Pip, her interested gaze on Pip's head. 'It's really very ginger, isn't it? Have you always been like that?'

Pip tensed, prepared to incur her employer's wrath by telling the elegant brunette exactly what she thought of her personal remarks, but was saved by the arrival of the man himself.

'Dearest!' Vanessa Clifton flung herself across the room but not, to Pip's surprise, into Hallam's arms. Instead, she laid a small hand on the sleeve of the surgeon's immaculate jacket, and gazed into his eyes. Even with the enormously high-heels she was wearing, she barely came to his chin.

'Miss . . . er, Miss,' she waved her hand vaguely in Pip's direction, 'your young lady was just entertaining me.'

'Good, good,' he replied, his gaze sweeping over Pip without enthusiasm. 'Just clear up will you, Miss Weston? Sir David isn't due until five-thirty and I'll attend to him.'

Pip, dismissed, choked back a pert remark, and merely nodded, only to have her dislike of the pair fuelled by Miss Clifton's stage whisper as they left the room: 'You were right, Hallam. She *is* quaint!'

Quaint, am I? *Quaint?* How dare he! Her fury was directed at the surgeon, not at the dainty brunette, who probably didn't know any better. So, Hallam Fielding, I am quaint, am I? An oddity, an ugly duckling. That's what it amounted to, she fumed, her hands moving of their own accord as she replaced magazines, then went through to the clinic itself to tidy there.

Was she really an ugly duckling? She found herself in front of the full-length mirror which adorned one wall of the clinic. Mr Fielding said it helped him to convince obese patients that they really *were* fat, showed them as they were.

Now, it showed Miss Philippa Weston as she was—a slightly built, waif-like figure with small breasts, a neat waist and slender legs that were long considering she was only five foot nothing. And that hair! Forlornly, she put a hand to her burning face. She *was* a carrot-top, there was no denying it. The evidence was there, in that hateful mirror.

With hands that trembled, she unpinned her hair, then gently unplaited it, and shook her head a couple of times until the rich tresses swung free.

Perhaps something could be salvaged if she had it cut and professionally shaped. It wouldn't appear quite so red then.

She had always been used to Melanie being the pretty one, the sister surrounded by admirers, but until now she hadn't thought of herself as quaint. She had had offers enough when she was doing her training. Though never the life and soul of the party, her quiet wit and gentle ways had been appreciated, and she hadn't lacked acquaintances.

'Am I really quaint?' She spoke aloud, then drew back, horrified, as another face appeared in the mirror. She had been told, as a child, that vain children who were always mirror-gazing would find the Devil at their shoulder one day, sharing the mirror with them, and it was true!

A dark head, a thin, clever face, and bleak dark eyes were there beside her. Only this was Hallam Fielding, and in her embarrassment she would have preferred Old Nick himself!

A friendly hand rested gently on her shoulder, as she saw Hallam Fielding shake his head. 'No, Pip, you aren't quaint. I have never said so—at least not in the way you think.'

Wide-eyed and wondering, she gazed back at his reflection, at the reflection of them both, standing side by side, the tall, greying surgeon and the slender redhead, seeming a mere slip of a girl beside the dignified Hallam.

'It's all right,' she managed, when she had recovered her breath. He'd called her Pip! 'I'm sure Miss Clifton didn't mean it unkindly.' Of course she did, Pip wanted to yell at him, but it would solve nothing. What use was a slanging match?

Yet, moments later, that was exactly what they

were having, for Pip went on, without thinking: 'I wonder if your brother considers me a quaint little soul, as well?' Now, why ever did I say *that*? she pondered. She wasn't the least bit interested in Geoffrey Fielding's opinion.

The surgeon's face darkened. 'Why don't you ask him?' he said bitterly. 'When you have time from leading him on!' Abruptly, he turned, but Pip wasn't going to let it go at that. Oh, no!

'When did I lead Dr Fielding on?' she asked, shakily.

A heavy brow was raised, and a sardonic gleam came to the dark grey eyes. 'You have been offering him all sorts of delights since he came!' he shot back at her, and she gasped.

'You sobbed on his shoulder the very minute he arrived!' he charged, unfairly. 'You lied to me about young Simon, just so both Geoffrey and I would feel sorry for you, lend you a shoulder to cry on at regular intervals. It wouldn't surprise me if you weren't scheming to marry young Geoff! Vanessa said he had his arm around you this morning when she passed. You appeared to be kissing, but she wasn't sure. She gave you the benefit of the doubt.'

Hands on hips, she sent him a look of such loathing that he should have died on the spot. 'That was very good of her, I must say! I'll thank her next time she drifts in here trailing perfume all over the place,' she almost choked, aware that she was jealous of the other girl, and hating herself for it.

'Vanessa always smells delightful,' he said, glaring back. A muscle twitched at the side of his jaw, and Pip saw how desperately tired he looked. He had been operating all morning, then seen patients all afternoon. She ought not to be subjecting him to an emotional scene. He should rest.

When she timidly said as much, it was his turn to be struck dumb. 'You work too hard,' she went on, defiantly. 'We shouldn't be arguing over a silly misunderstanding. Dr Fielding was removing a fly from my eye when Miss Clifton passed. That was the only occasion he put his arm around me,' she continued, forlornly, then risked another glance at his weary face.

'Why should you care how hard I work?' he asked, his tone gentle, and, numbly, she shook her head.

Why, indeed? She didn't want to probe too deeply for her reasons. She was mixed-up and did not fully understand why she should care one way or the other. As long as he didn't work so hard that he dropped dead and, therefore, did her out of a job, it was all that mattered.

'Do you care, Pip?' The surgeon insisted on knowing, and put a finger under her chin and gently forced her head back.

She eyed him, warily. What sort of trick was this? He accused her of flirting with his brother, yet now he was inviting her to flirt with him. And where was the glamorous Miss Clifton?

She was about to make some flippant remark, anything to lighten the intensity of the moment, but he didn't give her a chance. His searching mouth pressed hers, gently, sweetly, and she was lost.

Wonderingly, she went into his arms, and allowed him to stroke her slender body. Her senses were doing crazy things. She'd read of girls whose senses reeled at such moments but had never known quite what it meant. She did now!

She couldn't think straight, the air around them was exploding with beautiful stars, and she knew then: she loved him!

It was incredible, but it was the only thought in her head. Hallam's lips moved to her hair and he began to kiss it, murmuring softly all the while.

'Such lovely hair, pet,' he whispered.

Drawing back a little she asked, wonderingly: 'Is it? I thought I was a quaint carrot-head.' Some of the bitterness crept back into her voice, she couldn't help it, but he only laughed, before pulling her to him again.

'It's red-gold, Pip. The colour of a glorious sunrise.'

Sunrise. How beautiful, how expressive the word. Philippa of the sunrise hair, she thought, dreamily. In the sad times ahead, that remark was all she had to cling to.

'Oh, Pip!' His gentle lovemaking turned to something like desperation, as he bent his head and kissed her ear, her throat, where his lips lingered, teasing gently. With his tongue her forced open her already parted mouth, and eagerly, she begged for more.

His hands, with their delicate long fingers, slid down her body and rested on her buttocks, moulding her closer. Her body responded with a passion that was frightening in its intensity.

She ought to stop him, she knew, but then he trailed one finger expertly down the side of her breast, and she quivered. Her whole body was afire—surely there were no more delights to come? This was perfect! Utter rapture. Each movement, each insidious movement of that mouth, those hands was setting her alight.

She wanted to cry out words of love. I love you, Hallam! I want you! her heart cried, but her lips had to remain silent, except for a little moan as his lips once more claimed hers.

Then, unaccountably, he pushed her away, so suddenly that she stumbled and had to hang on to the examination couch for support.

Horrified, she watched the man she loved struggling to gain control of himself. He stood, slightly bent, his hands spread wide apart on the clinically white wall, as though he was holding it up. His breath came in deep, gulping sighs, and she went towards him, wanting only to soothe and comfort him.

'Leave me alone!' he bellowed, head still down. 'God! What have I done?'

Backing away, she said, shyly: 'You didn't do anything.'

'But I might have done!' A shudder ran through him, and she did so long to take him in her arms, tell him that whatever he did to her she would welcome, but of course she could not.

'A middle-aged man groping with a teenager,' he muttered, half to himself, and Pip's temper flared.

'I am *not* a teenager, I'm twenty!' she snapped. 'That is quite different! Anyway, you weren't groping, you were . . .' What could she say? That he was making love to a young woman he cared about? That he intended to marry her afterwards?

Pip was a realist. He wanted a woman and she just happened to be available. It could have been *any* woman, might have been Vanessa Clifton . . .

'Where *is* Miss Clifton?' she asked coldly, as his

breathing quietened.

He swore. 'Vanessa! I forgot all about her! I just came in . . .' He paused and shook his head, as if to clear it. 'I forget what I came in for, but it certainly wasn't for a big seduction scene,' he said, wryly, at last meeting her intense gaze.

The tormented grey eyes, now anything but cold, rested briefly on her face. 'I'm sorry. I don't know what came over me. A sudden rush of blood, perhaps.'

'That is perfectly all rigt, Mr Fielding,' she said, formally. 'I understand.'

The glacial look was back now, his expression distant. But this was the Hallam Fielding she knew and understood. She could cope with the clinical, autocratic consultant. It was the passionate, demanding man inside that threw her out of gear!

Her eyes followed his tall, lean figure to the door, and beyond. Miss Clifton's eager arms were waiting out there. *She* would know how to cope.

Once more, Pip gazed into the big mirror, but how different her reflection was this time! A stranger gazed back at her. A young woman with flushed face, starry eyes, and a cloud of rich red-gold hair that needed a good brushing. But she was no longer a carrot-top. Her hair was the colour of the morning sun, and she would never forget his words.

The rest of Pip's month's trial passed without further incident. Dr Geoffrey Fielding returned home to Yorkshire after his two-week break. He had remained friendly, and, once or twice, seemed about to linger and talk to her, but that was all. Hallam Fielding had no need to be concerned.

Aunt Norah seemed grudgingly to have accepted that Pip was there to stay, and became a bit more human. She even took an interest in the little boy, much to the sisters' amazement. Presumably her nephew had explained that Simon was Melanie's child, and that his parents were respectably married!

Pip's heart warmed to her. Probably the old lady was lonely and needed someone to love. But that was the only person for whom her heart thawed a little. Since the passionate session in the clinic she had carefully packed icicles around her heart. It would take a better man than Hallam Fielding to thaw her out again.

Her first reaction to men had been the correct one. They were all out for what they could get. They caused the women who loved them untold misery and heartbreak. Once they broke a woman's heart they stamped it into the ground for good measure, until there was nothing left but a blood-stain on the ground.

Pip had once read that African buffaloes treated their victims like that. Not content with merely killing them they had to extract every ounce of pleasure from the murder. It was almost human, Pip thought, shuddering. It *was* human, because that was what Hallam Fielding had done to her heart.

Since that time he had been nasty. Not just icily dismissive as previously, but actually nasty. Hateful. Everything he could find fault with, he did. She ought to have changed her typewriter ribbon days ago, it was far too light, he would thunder. Or she dressed improperly for the office, she must have an overall. So he went out and

bought her an overall, and she had gasped at sight
of it. If he could have found an uglier, more un-
becoming one, she would have been surprised. It
was a muddy sort of green, with large buttons, and
reached to well below her knees. It was unsightly,
and Pip was tempted to tell him to wear it himself,
but wisely held her tongue.

When Vanessa Clifton, who was a regular,
almost daily visitor now, saw it, she went off into
peals of laughter, then apologised graciously,
before laughing again.

Pip had stood her ground, and refused to be
baited, and Miss Clifton just *loved* baiting her. 'The
Carrot' was how she was heard to describe Pip to
Sister Farrell.

With her hair, and that green smock-like horror,
Pip supposed she did resemble a carrot. The sunrise
hair. How often she recalled those words, especially
when her boss was being particularly hateful to
her.

Now that Vanessa was around, he no longer
took Melanie out, and Pip was distressed at the
change in her sister. She became paler, quieter. She,
the once-extrovert Melanie!

It was pitiful to see the change, and it was one
more reason for Pip to hate Hallam Fielding.
Melanie had been hurt twice now, once by her lazy
husband, and then by her sister's employer.

Men were pigs, savages! Pip hated all men, because of her mother and her sister's heartbreak,
but she mentally stuck pins in a wax effigy of
Hallam. For him, she reserved her most intense
feelings. As before, she was aware how narrow was
the border between love and hate, but was firmly
convinced that the emotion that rose into her

breast whenever he appeared was pure hate. There could never be anything else between them, no matter how much his expert seductive powers stirred her unawakened body.

No mention was made of Pip being asked to leave at the end of her month, and she was surprised as well as relieved. Though as she managed both the job *and* Aunt Norah Tester well enough, she supposed he couldn't be bothered to readvertise the post.

Then Miss Tester dropped her bombshell. She was placidly knitting some six weeks after Pip's arrival. The television was on full, as she was hard of hearing and resolutely refused a television hearing adjuster.

Pip winced as what passed for music blared out at her. It was physically painful and doing no good to her eardrums, but no matter. If she went deaf who would care, anyway?

'Next month!' Miss Tester finished, triumphantly, and Pip stared. Had she missed something of importance?

Ignoring Miss Tester's protests, she turned down the sound, and apologised for not hearing before. 'Is there something interesting happening next month?' She tried to sound enthusiastic, but could not. The old lady's nephew had been particularly sarcastic that afternoon, and had written all over Pip's carefully-typed letters so that she had to re-type them at double quick speed while he almost stood over her.

At least he had stayed in the room, one immaculate hand tapping impatiently on the arm of his chair while he waited. When they were finished, he had signed them after a cursory read, grunted something that might have been 'Thanks', and hurried out.

She knew where he was going, of course, for she'd had to book the best seats in the theatre for him and a guest. No need to puzzle out the name of the guest! They were going to see the new musical, one that Pip wanted to see. True, there was no reason why she couldn't have gone, but by herself it wouldn't have been any fun. Nothing was fun any more. She was simply existing from day to day. Something had to happen, to change, or she would go mad.

'It is in Cornwall,' Miss Tester finished, and Pip flushed. Once again she hadn't been listening.

'That will be nice, Miss Tester,' Pip answered brightly. 'What did you say it was called?'

Miss Tester sighed, impatiently. 'Have you heard a word I said, child?' she asked, her gaze shrewd, and Pip shook her head.

'I'm sorry. I've had a bad day but that's no excuse for not listening, I know,' Pip hastened to add, as Miss Tester compressed her thin lips.

'No excuse at all,' the woman agreed. 'Has my nephew been more difficult than usual?'

Pip kept her eyes on her tightly clasped hands, then, absently, began to twist her mother's ring round and round. It was a habit she had when distraught. 'Sometimes he is unbearable,' she admitted, and his aunt snorted.

'Don't tell *me* what he's like! He is a widower, you know,' she continued, changing the subject.

Surprised, Pip glanced up, and was just in time to catch a strange expression in the old lady's grey eyes before they became bland again.

'I didn't know. Has he any children? He never

mentions any.' Not that he would make a good father, she thought, resentfully. He was far too much the perfectionist.

Miss Tester shook her head. 'Patricia never wanted any. She loathed children. Wasn't the slightest bit domesticated. She was one of those prissy women who faint at sight of a spot of blood!' she said, disparagingly. 'It was "Patricia doesn't like this" or "That would never do for Patricia" and so on.' Miss Tester waved a beringed hand, and Pip smiled. 'She was tall and blonde. Out of a bottle, I shouldn't wonder. And that voice! He likes children. Do you?' Miss Tester asked, veering suddenly away from the subject of the late Mrs Fielding.

Pip nodded. 'I love babies. He thought Simon was mine, you know!' she cried, suddenly remembering yet another grievance to chalk up against the surgeon.

'So did I!' Miss Tester admitted, and Pip covered the wrinkled hand with her own.

'Sometimes I think he's nastier since he found out that Simon belongs to Melanie,' Pip went on, reflectively. It was true. He resented Melanie having a child because he fancied her. He didn't want the responsibility of someone else's child.

Yet there was Vanessa Clifton. He didn't care that deeply for Melanie, it seemed.

'So what will you do now?' Miss Tester asked, out of the blue, and Pip stared. 'No, no, I forgot. You weren't listening, were you?' Miss Tester stared into space for a moment, and Pip gazed at her, a frown marring the smoothness of her brow. What was it she'd said about Cornwall? Was she going for a long holiday?

'I shall be going to live with my niece, Hallam's sister. She lives near Truro.'

'Permanently?' Now she was getting to know the woman better, Pip liked her and was sorry to hear about the move. She was gradually learning to cope with Miss Tester's eccentricities.

'I expect so. You won't have my trying little ways to put up with, at least!'

'You aren't *that* trying!' Pip said, mischievously. 'I expect Mr Fielding will find enough work to keep me busy. He does, anyway.'

'Yes, but there is Alison.'

'Alison?' Surely not another girl-friend?

'My niece Elizabeth's daughter. She has just graduated and Hallam promised her the flat.'

'But . . .' Pip began to protest, but was waved down.

'That was when she started at university. Long before he thought of offering accommodation with the job. He's had to now because we are so isolated here. Jessie Farrell fortunately lives just down the road with her sister, but Hallam can't always expect to get staff locally. They are mainly stock-broker type people around here, or the horsey types,' Miss Tester said.

'But I've got the flat now!' Pip wailed. 'He can't turn me out! Can he?'

Miss Tester laid a comforting hand on Pip's shoulder, and Pip was genuinely touched. Sympathetic gestures in this household were few and far between. 'I really don't know what he intends. You must ask him. Is there nowhere else your sister and nephew could stay?'

Pip shook her head, her expression set. It was serious. If he meant to turn her out of the flat it must mean dismissal from the job, too. Or she would give notice. There was no alternative.

There was another blow for Pip the next day. It was lunchtime, the morning had been easy because Mr Fielding was operating all day. She was almost happy as she typed. The sun streamed in the window, giving the dismal room a holiday air.

Because she knew she would be alone, she'd discarded the dreadful green overall and worn a blue and white striped cotton tee-shirt with a white flared skirt. The overall, apart from being dowdy, was also dreadfully hot.

The white skirt had a fashionable split at the sides, and she wore no tights. Even her sandals were temporarily laid aside.

Bare-footed and bare-legged, she made her way up the steps to the flat, even managing to whistle a little tune.

The problem of the flat had to be solved, but so optimistic was her mood that she felt Mr Fielding would be reasonable and offer them some other accommodation. There was plenty of room in the old house, and she was speculating which rooms he might offer them, when Melanie confronted her at the door.

Melanie's face was set and determined, and all sorts of thoughts raced through Pip's mind as she stared at her sister. 'Something's wrong with Simon? Is it?' Pip gripped her sister by the upper arms, willing her to speak.

'No, he's fine. But we're leaving.'

Pip looked blank. 'There isn't anywhere else to go. Or did you hear about the niece?'

It was Melanie's turn to look blank. 'What niece? Never mind, I don't care. We are going back to

Peter.' Melanie's chin rose defiantly, and the sisters traded glances.

'Melanie, you can't!' Pip shook her head, sadly, already knowing it was useless. Melanie would always be a fool where Peter was concerned.

'I can and I will!' Melanie snapped, her lovely face distraught. 'Pip, I love him! You wouldn't understand,' she went on, and Pip wanted to yell back at her: 'Of course I understand! I've loved and hated, too! I hate this man but I can't live without him.'

Yes, perhaps Melanie could not live without her husband. Pip knew the feeling only too well, now—miserable together but even more so apart.

'When are you going?' she asked, dully, staring without enthusiasm at the salad Melanie had prepared.

'Today. The taxi is coming at three. I'll be there when he gets in from work.'

Melanie, too, stared at the food, then glanced at Pip, eyes wary. 'Haven't you anything else to say? No more objections?'

Pip shook her head. 'Are you sure you'll be all right?'

Melanie nodded, still staring at her plate. 'I have to try again, Pip. You *do* understand?'

'Yes.' Pip had been about to tell her sister about Mr Fielding's niece turning them out of the flat, but what did it matter now?

Melanie had a home to go to and Mr Fielding could give Pip a room in his house. Somewhere large enough to turn into a bed-sit.

Hungrily, she looked around the room. This was better than a bed-sit! Why, oh why, couldn't she stay here?

In the few weeks since she had joined the surgeon's staff she had come to look on the flat as home. Although it was small, and filled with furniture not her own, to Pip it was the closest she'd been to a home since her mother died.

One room in the main building wouldn't be the same, but in the circumstances, did she need to stay with Hallam Fielding?

The same thought must have crossed her sister's mind, for Melanie said, suddenly: 'You could leave, as well. Couldn't you? There is no reason to stay here now that you don't need a whole flat.'

Pip raised a brow. 'Just where would I go?'

Melanie shrugged, 'You're single, you can find somewhere.'

'Thank you,' Pip said, drily. She forbore to remind Melanie that it was *her* fault Pip was saddled with an unreasonable employer, and about to be deprived of her accommodation. It didn't matter. Probably Hallam Fielding would use the flat as an excuse to get rid of her altogether.

After an unsatisfactory lunch-break, Pip went back to the office, no longer whistling cheerfully. Her head ached. She might feel better if she cried, but tears would come later, if at all. Mr Fielding's letters had to be typed ready for his return this evening. Then Miss Tester needed help with her packing, for she was going the following Monday.

The grey-haired housekeeper Pip had seen on her first day came in daily, to do the housework, take messages, etc. In addition, she and her daughter-in-law prepared most meals for the surgeon and his aunt, other than breakfast, so they were kept busy. Neither of them would have time to help the old lady with her sorting-out, and Miss Tester had a great deal to be packed.

Still bare-footed, Pip swung open the office-door, her head bent, feeling that all the sorrows of the world were upon her shoulders, then she gasped.

Hallam Fielding swung round. He had been staring out at the garden. There were lines of fatigue around his eyes and mouth, and Pip longed to smooth them away.

They eyed each other, warily. Pip waited for the death sentence to fall. She knew one thing. Far better to endure Hallam's sarcastic tongue and domineering ways than to leave. She could not leave. She *would* not.

'Aunt Norah says she told you,' Hallam said, flatly, his dark gaze going back to the garden.

Pip's anger rose. He couldn't even be bothered to look at her! 'I didn't expect you back for lunch,' she said, inconsequently.

The grey brooding eyes came to rest on her. 'Is that relevant, Miss Weston?'

'No,' she muttered, staring at the desk. 'She told me. She said you need the flat for your niece.'

'Mm. I did promise it to her. She's doing some research job and there isn't anywhere else she can stay. She is getting married, as well, and isn't going to forget that I offered free accommodation!'

'No.'

'You can move into the house,' he offered, without enthusiasm.

'What about Miss Clifton? *She* won't like that!' Pip flung at him, feeling spiteful.

'No, she probably won't.' Hallam sounded amused. It was all right for him. *He* didn't have to put up with Miss Clifton's sharp tongue and nasty habit of calling Pip 'Carrot'.

'Melanie is leaving.' Pip dropped her bombshell, but it fell flat.

'I know. She told me she might.'

'But she's only just told me!' Pip wailed, eyes wide.

'Do you always come to work bare-foot?' he asked, suddenly, his glance going to her brown legs and feet.

Pip gazed down at them. 'I didn't expect you back.' she said, defensively.

'No, so you said.' There was a quiet irony in his voice, and Pip flushed.

'If I had known, I would have worn that dreadful overall!' she flung at him, as he continued to stare. She was becoming more embarrassed by the minute. Surely he didn't believe she was trying to lead him on? He had no business returning so early!

'That outfit suits you better than the overall,' he admitted, then passed a hand wearily across his eyes. 'If Melanie is definitely going back to her husband, that puts a different complexion on things,' he said, looking up.

His eyes were cold, iron-grey, and Pip quivered. He was going to fire her! Well, she wouldn't go!

She drew herself up, and faced him, resolutely. Let him just try to get rid of her!

'Will you marry me, Pip?'

Pip stared, her eyes growing bigger and rounder. Surely she had mis-heard? Hallam Fielding, eminent consultant, wasn't proposing to little Pip Weston. Was he?

Her pretty mouth opened, then closed again, as Hallam moved towards her.

CHAPTER FIVE

NERVOUSLY Pip took a step backwards, her eyes mirroring her shock and uncertainty.

'For God's sake, child!' Hallam exploded. 'I'm not going to rape you!'

Pip went crimson. 'I . . .' she began, then looked helplessly at him.

He gave a wry smile. 'You look about fifteen in that outfit,' he commented. 'Cradle-snatching, that's what I'm doing.'

She found her voice at last. 'Why?' she croaked out, and he appeared surprised by the question.

'I should have thought it was obvious. Do you need an involved explanation?'

'No, but . . .'

'We can't discuss it here, Pip. I have a full list this afternoon. We can go somewhere quiet this evening. I'll pick you up about eight.'

'Yes, but . . .' she tried again, but the enigmatic Hallam Fielding had gone. Shaken, she almost fell into the easy-chair. Marriage! She was going to be married to Mr Fielding!

She giggled. Fancy calling your fiancé Mr Fielding! She was going to marry Hallam. She felt light-headed. Once, at a hospital party, she'd drunk three glasses of sherry and gone giggly. Then she had started to cry, and all the while her head seemed to be floating far above her body.

That was how she felt now. She, little Philippa Weston, was going to become Mrs Hallam

Fielding! It was incredible, unbelievable.

She sobered. Yes, unbelievable was the correct word. *Why* did he propose?

Now she'd recovered from the shock, the elation died down. Practical Miss Weston was nobody's fool, even if Hallam thought she was. She bit her lower lip savagely, drawing a speck of blood.

He had no accommodation to offer her except in his house. With Aunt Norah gone and Melanie returning, if only temporarily, to her husband, there was no-one else living in the house. True, the niece would be in the flat, but that wasn't the same thing at all.

Hallam Fielding had a reputation to worry about. It would never do if his wealthy patients knew he had a secretary sharing his home. They would jump to their own conclusions, regardless of the truth.

He was protecting her reputation as well as his own by offering her marriage. That was all.

Hallam's wife! Her heart began to flutter as the wider implications hit her. Sharing Hallam's name, his life, his bed . . .

Wide-eyed, she stared at nothing in particular, a tiny smile hovering about her lips. To be held in his arms, feel those long, sensitive fingers on her body, caressing her . . . Oh, she couldn't bear it! Hallam, I love you! she called out, silently, all her high ideals about never being a man's slave rushing out the window. He would be annoyed when he found out she was inexperienced. She understood him to that extent. A perfectionist himself, he expected perfection in others. Yet surely he would make allowances for her inexperience, her youth?

She would make him happy. She would wait on him hand and foot, if that was what pleased him.

No Eastern potentate could boast a more willing slave!

While she was searching, unsuccessfully, for something to wear for the evening, she remembered Vanessa Clifton, and what remained of her excitement died within.

Vanessa *said* she was Hallam Fielding's fiancée. She didn't wear an engagement ring, true, but that meant nothing.

Pip sat down heavily on the edge of her bed, a lonely figure now that Melanie had gone. It was Melanie who had taken the pretty brown dress that Pip needed for her dinner-date.

Loss of the dress was nothing beside the awful implications. Even in his anxiety to protect his good name, he could hardly have overlooked his current fiancée. *No-one* could overlook Vanessa Clifton! By comparison, Pip believed herself to be mundane, a dowdy, quaint little figure with nothing special to commend her to a man such as Hallam.

If he married Vanessa straight away, *then* he could offer Pip a few rooms in his house. It would be perfectly respectable. Possibly the elegant brunette made too many demands on him and that was why he preferred Pip. Whatever his reason, she assured herself, she would do her best to become a suitable wife for the surgeon.

In the end, she had to make do with her very ordinary blue over-dress. She had nothing else suitable to wear, and was ashamed of her appearance. Probably Hallam would be ashamed of her, too. Already she had let him down, and they weren't even officially engaged yet!

She wore her cream silk blouse under the dress,

and swept her unruly hair back and up into an elegant chignon. She had no makeup other than a lipstick, for Melanie had taken it, and she applied the lipstick sparingly. There was no point in trying to appear sophisticated, like someone out of a fashion salon. She was still plain little Pip and the surgeon must accept her as she was.

When he appeared, some ten minutes late, she was dismayed. He looked every inch the successful, moneyed businessman. The cut of his dark lounge suit was faultless, his tie discreet. Gold cufflinks were just visible, and she had no doubt they were expensive.

By comparison, she felt a dowdy little bluebird. The over-dress wasn't entirely suitable for evening, but she had few clothes. Mrs Noakes had never paid well, and although she received an excellent salary from Hallam, a lot of it went to Melanie. Pip felt her sister deserved a few treats, some extra clothes; certainly the little boy did. He would have had no toys at all if Pip's money hadn't provided them. Daddy's money went on drink and, probably, other women, though Melanie didn't seem to think her husband would be unfaithful. Pip thought otherwise.

Hallam did not comment on her appearance, but from the slight tightening of his hard mouth Pip knew he was disappointed in her, annoyed that she hadn't taken the trouble to dress correctly for the evening.

He had probably never been poor, Pip thought resentfully, as he courteously handed her into the shining limousine. He didn't understand that there were more important items to spend money on than clothes.

If Hallam was disappointed in Pip, she certainly wasn't disappointed in the restaurant he had chosen. It was a huge, glass palace ablaze with lights, and her eyes brightened. Dining out was a rare enough treat, but this ... this was out of this world! She was being spoilt. For one so young, she had a veneer of cynicism, and suspected that after the marriage Hallam wouldn't take her anywhere as special as this. He might not take her out at all, she mused, giving him a vague smile as they went down to the lower floor.

No, she would be expected to cook, clean, still be his general office help, as well as entertain his colleagues. A tall order, but he was at least providing her with a home. And his love. Well, no, she conceded, he didn't love her, but at least they would have a satisfactory marriage.

She loved him. Her love must do for them both. Oh, Hallam! her heart cried, I *will* make you happy! Just be kind to me, that's all I ask.

She must have muttered some of her thoughts aloud because Hallam stared, irritation written all over his hard face, and she coloured. Oh, please let him be kind! she wailed inwardly. At the moment he looked positively forbidding.

The soup came and went, without Pip noticing whether or not it had any taste. She was too over-wrought to bother much about food. She was desperate to hear Hallam repeat his proposal, to know the conditions. She was also trying to pluck up the courage to ask about Vanessa.

'Some wine, Pip?'

'What? Oh, yes, please!' she said, with forced enthusiasm.

He poured a generous measure of white wine.

Pip tasted it and found it too dry. Not wanting to make a fuss she drank it steadily, unaware that she should have taken only lady-like sips between the conversation.

'Trying to fortify yourself, Pip?' His tone was annoyed, and she gazed at her empty glass in dismay. She was always doing the wrong thing. Would she ever please him?

Without her asking, he refilled her glass, then his own. The fish arrived then, and although Pip couldn't identify it, the sauce tasted of mushrooms and garlic, and was delicious.

She sat back, replete, and assured Hallam she had enjoyed every mouthful. When he made no comment, she took another sip of wine and thanked him, over-sweetly, for the meal. She felt there ought to be a pudding but perhaps he was economising. If he was dining out with Vanessa he certainly would not stint *her*, but that was irrelevant now.

'The meal isn't over yet,' he said, sternly, deftly removing her glass which was still half-full. 'I have ordered steak. Then there is a light pudding to follow, or cheese and biscuits if you prefer?'

Embarrassed because she'd thought the meal was over, and flushed with too much wine, Pip grew restless. 'Nice of you to ask me which I would prefer!'

'Pip!' He spoke softly yet with all the authority behind the word of one who was accustomed to obedience, but she went on, heedless of the danger: 'I don't happen to like steak. But it never occurred to you to ask, did it? I bet you always ask Vanessa Clifton what *she* wants!'

Eyes bright with temper and unshed tears, Pip

stared him out. Or tried to, but in the end she was the one to drop her gaze.

'You are nothing but a spoilt juvenile,' he said, irritably, still keeping his voice low. 'I must be out of my mind!' he went on, more to himself than her.

'Perhaps you are,' she agreed, as the steak appeared. 'We were going to discuss your . . . proposition,' she carried on, once the waiter had drifted away on unseen wheels.

'Ah, yes, my proposition,' he said dryly. 'It think it inadvisable that you should share my home. There will be just the two of us now that Melanie's gone.'

She nodded, slowly. 'You have your reputation to think of.'

'And yours,' he rebuked her. 'I was considering you, as well.'

'Decent of you,' she put in, tartly, then could have bitten out her tongue as his face darkened with the anger that was always there, under the surface.

'In the circumstances, I decided I would offer you marriage,' he continued. 'You would also be more readily available.'

She opened her mouth in surprise but he didn't appear to notice. 'Sister Farrell will be retiring next spring. There seems no reason why she couldn't train you to assume her duties.'

She turned her shocked gasp into a cough, and furiously stabbed the steak with her knife, wishing it was Hallam's back. More readily available, indeed! So now she was to be clinic nurse on top of everything else.

'What about Vanessa Clifton?' she asked, and was pleased to see his discomfiture.

'She presumed too much,' he replied, after a lengthy silence.

'She told me she was your fiancée. You must have asked her,' Pip pointed out coldly.

'No, I did not! She took it for granted.'

'If she was your mistress I suppose she might assume you would marry her one day,' she said, giving the offending steak another stab, and taking pleasure in doing so.

'For God's sake, Pip! Stop throwing poison darts at me and behave like an adult!'

The stormy-grey eyes bored into hers, and hastily she ate a minute piece of steak. It tasted like rubber.

'Leave the steak if it isn't to your liking. I'll order something else.' He turned to beckon the waiter, but she stopped him in time.

Both of them gazed down at her small hand which she'd laid intimately on his arm. Blushing, she removed it. She had no right . . . But of course, she had a right! She was going to be Hallam's bride!

Defiantly, she said: 'I'll eat the vegetables, then have the pudding. Next time you bring me, I would like roast lamb or chicken, thank you very much!'

'Salty tonight, aren't you?' He sounded amused, much to her relief.

The pudding was a light sponge overflowing with fruit and topped by lashings of cream, and Pip licked her lips, hungrily.

Hallam put his head back and laughed at her pleasure. Glad she'd done something right, she joined in the laughter, then eagerly tucked into the sponge.

'Naturally it will be a business proposition.'

The last mouthful of sponge turned to sawdust, as he continued, believing she hadn't understood: 'It will be a marriage in name only. I wouldn't dream of making any demands on a girl of your age,' he said, staring at the wall behind her.

'No, naturally,' she said quietly, surprised that she could find her voice. She wasn't good enough to take to bed; oh, no, all Pip was good for was to be an unpaid skivvy while he got his sexual pleasure elsewhere. 'I wonder what Geoff will say,' she continued brightly, hoping for some reaction.

'Geoff?' Hallam said blankly, and she nodded.

'Won't he be surprised! He never imagined me as a sister-in-law, you know.'

The barb went home, and she got a reaction, though not perhaps what she had expected. His steely fingers closed over her wrist, and she squealed with the pain.

'Don't speak of my brother in that way again,' he almost snarled, and she struggled to hide her triumph. He cared! He must do, to get so hot under the collar about Geoffrey. Then his next words dashed even that hope.

'I'm fond of young Geoffrey. He's ten years younger than me and I feel responsible for him in some ways. If you imagine you can play one of us off against the other, you can think again! I won't have Geoff used in that way! Do you hear, Pip?' He shook the wrist he was still holding, and she nodded.

Yes, she heard. Message received and understood. It was Geoffrey he cared about, not her. He didn't care if Pip's feelings were hurt, so long as she didn't upset his brother.

They didn't linger over coffee. Now the main

business of the evening was over he seemed eager
to return home.

Pip acknowledged that he must be desperately
weary. He'd had a full day at the hospital and
would probably write up some notes tonight. Of
course he was eager to go. She couldn't help wishing, though, that he cared for her just a little. If
Hallam Fielding felt for her even one-quarter of
what she felt for him, she would be satisfied. She'd
learned to make do with very little. But it was clear
his motives were selfish. With marriage to Pip, he
would gain a clinic nurse, a general secretary, a
cook, housekeeper, washer of shirts, slave . . . and
all for free. That Pip might have feelings on the
matter did not occur to him.

With an effort she kept back the tears, though
she felt sure her heart was visibly breaking.

'I'll show you over the house,' he announced, on
their return. 'You haven't seen it all, have you?'

'No, only Miss Tester's quarters,' she said,
quietly, so quietly that he glanced at her sharply.

'I thought now that I've set your mind at rest,
you would be happy,' he commented. The grey eyes
were concerned, and she managed a wan smile. He
must never suspect the depth of her feelings.

'What was it you set my mind at rest about?' she
said, ungrammatically, and a tender smile briefly
crossed his lean face.

'About us. About it being on a business-like
basis, of course. I thought that was what was
bothering you earlier.'

'Oh, no,' she answered, truthfully, 'it wasn't
bothering me at all.'

'Good, good. I'll show you your new quarters.'
Taking her firmly by the hand, he led her upstairs,

unaware of the poignancy of his action.

Upstairs to my room, *our* room, she thought.
Just as if we are going to be a normal married
couple. Can't you see I love you, Hallam? she
wanted to scream. Are you so dense where other
people's emotions are concerned? Can't you tell?

Nothing of the intensity of her feelings showed
as she inspected the double bedroom with adjoining
bathroom that he had already earmarked for
her use. So they were not even going to share a
room!

She liked the old house. It had character written
all over it, from the white-painted five-bar entrance
gate, to the big, old-fashioned wash-house that
overlooked the rockery.

Her bedroom was at the front, overlooking the
gravelled drive and with a view to the main road
and the hills beyond. It was a treble rather than a
double room, and there was plenty of room for
two in the bed. Or would be, she corrected herself,
sourly, if the room was intended for an ordinary
bride.

She had never been in that part of 'White Gables'
before and had assumed the house to be smaller
than it actually was. Hallam told her there were six
bedrooms altogether, four with small bathrooms
adjoining, plus his study, the sitting-room where
she and Miss Tester often sat in the evenings, kitchen, wash-house and verandah, and the office and
clinical part she knew so well.

'One of the small bedrooms could be made over
into a sitting-room for you, I suppose,' Hallam
said, as the tour came to an end where it started—
in her new bedroom.

'There is a sitting-room already,' she pointed

out, determined not to lose her temper, and he merely shrugged.

Avoiding the bed, with its beautiful snow-white lace coverlet, she let her eyes roam the room. Pink and gold striped paper covered three walls, the fourth being a pale green, which blended well. There were two big wardrobes with fitted dressing-table, two other sets of drawers, and an easy chair. All modern. She would have liked something antique from downstairs, but perhaps that could be arranged later.

'Everything to your liking?' Hallam asked, hovering in the doorway, and she nodded, without enthusiasm. If she appeared too satisfied, he would cease trying to please her. She would, too soon, become part of the furniture, but there was no point in hurrying it.

On an impulse she tried the bed, ignoring Hallam, who leant against the door-post, his expression blank. It was very comfortable. She kicked off her shoes so as not to damage the beautiful coverlet, then bounced up and down a few times, pretending that she'd forgotten Hallam's presence. She would *make* him take notice of her! She would!

She lay back against the lace-trimmed pillow shams, and closed her eyes. It was heavenly. She hadn't realised she was so tired. All thoughts of enticing Hallam to join her flew away as she drifted off to sleep.

The light was out when she awoke, and she sat up, panic-stricken. She was in an unfamiliar room, on a strange bed. Then her clutching fingers felt the delicate lace, and she remembered. This was to be her room once she became the surgeon's bride.

Feeling foolish at her panic, she groped around

for the light. It was two a.m. and high time she was back in the flat. She doubted that Miss Tester would approve of the forthcoming marriage, and most certainly would not approve if she knew Pip had spent the night on her bridal bed.

When she crept downstairs, Pip saw light gleaming from the slightly ajar door of Hallam's study. She ought to tell him she was leaving so he could bolt the doors after her.

But he was alseep, and her heart softened. He'd removed his shoes, jacket and tie, and unbuttoned his shirt. There was a tantalising glimpse of black hair on his chest, reaching down to the waist-band of his trousers. His face was calm in sleep, a lock of hair falling over one eye.

She hated to disturb him, then decided she would not. She didn't want to spend a lonely night in the flat, and the courtyard after dark wasn't at all inviting. There might be prowlers . . .

Having convinced herself that there were strange men prowling out there, it was but a step more to decide that she would spend the night there, with the man she loved. There was no point in creeping up to the bedroom again. In any case, her practical mind argued, the bedclothes would need airing. It was far more sensible to sleep in the study. Warmer, too. Having won the argument with herself, she settled down in the easy-chair opposite Hallam, tucking her legs beneath her even though she would get cramp. She used his discarded jacket as a cover, and was perfectly snug.

She fell asleep with a smile on her lips, only to be awakened moments later, when she was gripped roughly by the arms and almost hurled to the ground.

Startled, she looked up into the angry, set face of the surgeon. Words trembled on her lips but he gave her no chance to explain.

'Will you get out of my study!' He spoke quietly, but there was no mistaking the venom in his tone. 'What are you going to do? Threaten to have me up for rape so you can collect a nice fat rake-off?'

'What?' Astonished, she struggled to rise, but he unceremoniously pushed her down again.

'That's where you belong, in the gutter!' he snapped, face livid. 'I offered you marriage. What else do you want?'

'N ... nothing, nothing at all,' she babbled, frightened at the strange light in his eyes. 'I didn't want to go out in the dark!' she whimpered. 'So ... so I saw the light and ...'

'And thought you would entice me tonight!' he finished for her.

Wonderingly, she shook her head. 'No, I'm tired.'

'I suppose you have a headache as well? But, no, *that* comes after the honeymoon, doesn't it?' he went on bitterly.

She put a hand beseechingly on his leg, for that was all she could reach of him.

'Please don't hurt me, H ... Hallam,' she begged. 'I ...' She almost said 'I love you' but bit her tongue in time. She didn't know why he had suddenly turned on her, but if he knew she loved him she would be completely at his mercy. He would use the knowledge against her. She didn't doubt that for a moment.

'You disgust me!' he flung at her, as she gazed appealingly up at him. 'I offered you marriage on a civilised basis. I expected, in return, a civilised, adult wife. If you are going to play tricks like this, I won't marry you!' He bit off each word as though speaking caused him pain, and cold fury took the place of the love in Pip's heart.

Scrambling up without his assistance, she faced him, hands on hips, red hair tumbling out of the chignon. 'I hate you! I don't want to marry you! I've got feelings, too!' she spat out. 'Hasn't it occurred to you I might fall in love someday, or might already *be* in love?'

He stepped back as though she had struck him, then ran long fingers through his already untidy hair. All the fight seemed knocked out of him, and she longed to take back her words.

He would assume she meant Geoffrey, not him. She had hurt him, and there was no way she could make amends.

'It hadn't occurred to me that you might be in love,' he acknowledged, levelly. 'Personally, I don't consider you are emotionally old enough to know the meaning of the word. In any case, Geoff is far too good for you. You *will* marry me, Pip. Leave Geoff alone. He'll get over it. Now get out.'

He gathered up his jacket and tie, replaced his shoes and brushed past her. 'I'll see you across to the flat, then lock up,' he called.

Miserably, she followed. There was only one idea in her mind. She *would* marry him, then make his life the misery he'd already made hers. She would suffer, too, but it would be worth it.

Oh, yes, Hallam Fielding, it would be worth it! He would come to share her hell on earth—a hell he had created.

CHAPTER SIX

THE wedding was a quiet affair a few weeks later. Pip, glancing around the small register office, couldn't believe it was happening. She was being married, joined in holy wedlock to the man she loved, adored and hated. And he would never know the depths of her feelings.

She stole a glance at the tall, austere figure by her side. He seemed so calm, so still. It wasn't the first time for him of course. Aunt Norah said his wedding to Patricia had been a big affair, with three hundred guests, many of them distinguished, and champagne bubbling everywhere. And the wedding gifts! Aunt Norah said royalty would have been delighted with some of them—exquisite china, porcelain figures which Patricia collected, a diamond set in stone intended as a paper-weight. Both families were rich, and Patricia had been an only child.

Wistfully, Pip fixed her eyes on the small spray of white flowers on the Registrar's desk, the only flowers in the room apart from the artificial rose pinned to the prayer book she carried. Not even the bridegroom wore a buttonhole.

Apart from Hallam and herself, there was only Aunt Norah Tester of the family there. Pip had wanted to invite Melanie, had gone so far as to beg to do so, but adamantly her husband-to-be had refused. It must be a quiet affair, with no fuss. Peter was over fond of alcohol, and if he got drunk and there was a scene, the publicity would be bad for Hallam's career.

Yes, we must think about Hallam's career, she mused, sourly. Nothing else matters. One thing to be grateful for—Melanie and Peter had settled their differences and were trying to make a go of it. But, oh, Pip *did* want Melanie by her side. She and Simon were Pip's only family now—except that she had acquired a husband, she recalled in some surprise.

The ceremony was over and she hadn't taken anything in. It was a dream, a nightmare from which there would be no awakening. Savagely, she brushed a few crumbs from the cream silk dress and jacket. The reception was as dull as the ceremony, with only sherry or spirits to drink. Even the wedding cake was a bought one that Sister Farrell had iced and decorated herself. A miniature bride and groom perched on top of the two-layer cake, hand in hand.

Riddled with self-pity, she didn't notice Miss Tester standing by her side until she spoke: 'Try to appear happy, Pip. This *is* your special day.'

Touched, Pip nodded, not trusting herself to speak.

'Hallam should have made more effort,' his Aunt said, testily. 'He could have ordered champagne, at least.'

'No,' Pip whispered. 'It isn't a special day for him—he's merely saving money. Getting a secretary for free now.'

'Pip!' Her new aunt sounded horrified, and moved away, smiling at Hallam's opposite number on the medical side.

He had invited one or two senior colleagues to

the reception, and Pip felt curious eyes on her from time to time. They were speculating, wondering, but unfailingly polite when they spoke to her. What, they were asking themselves, is Hallam Fielding doing marrying *her*? Pip didn't blame them. She wondered the same thing herself. But for their sake, she put a bright face on, smiling until her jaw muscles ached, pretending to a quiet contentment she did not feel.

One of them, Sir Peter, moved purposefully towards her now, and her eyes searched desperately for somewhere to hide. He had smiled distantly at her when they were introduced but hadn't spoken, apart from the usual conventional greetings. A tall, burly figure, he was closing in on her, eyes bright behind rimless spectacles, his high, domed forehead damp with perspiration.

What could she say to him? Perhaps he was going, and wanted to say a few parting words, but no. Sir Peter collected another glass of whisky on his way over, then beamed down at Pip.

'Time we had a talk, young lady,' he said, firmly steering her to a small settee. The reception was at White Gables itself, and that was the only cheering part for her. She felt at home here now.

'I think Hallam is . . .' he began and Pip cut him short.

'You think Hallam is making a ghastly mistake!' she finished, blue eyes stormy, daring him to contradict her.

One almost white brow was raised in astonishment, and Pip felt small. She ought not to speak her mind like that. Hallam was right, she *was* a juvenile, twenty-one on Christmas Eve, yet behaving like a twelve-year-old.

Contrite, she began to apologise, but Sir Peter waved her apologies away. 'No need, my dear. No need. I understand it must seem a quiet, cheap do after the other one. You heard about Patricia's reception?'

Bleakly, she nodded. 'I'm glad it's quiet,' she assured him. 'I couldn't take too many strangers yet.'

'I know.' The consultant patted her hand. 'She was a distant cousin of mine—Patricia, I mean.'

'Oh! Was she ... was she beautiful?' Pip asked, real interest in her voice for the first time. She was beginning to become envious of the late Mrs Fielding, even while knowing how stupid it was. If she could learn about Patricia, she could learn more about Hallam. She didn't know him at all. He was a perfectionist, a hard-working surgeon, had an abominable temper, didn't take sugar in his tea, and that was the sum total of her knowledge. Marriage to the perfect stranger.

There was a lengthy pause while he considered the question and he seemed reluctant to answer. Probably Patricia was so lovely he didn't like to offend Pip. He needn't have worried. Quaint little Pip would get over it, she thought, then felt a photograph being thrust into her hand.

It was a wedding photograph, of a younger, thinner Hallam and a tall blonde. Pip darted a look at Sir Peter, and he nodded.

'She *was* beautiful,' he conceded, but that was something she could see for herself. It was a close-up, head and shoulders, down to waist-level. Hallam was gazing adoringly at his bride, whose delicate bone-structure and lustrous hair could have earned her a fortune as a model.

Pip felt tears pricking her eyelids. Such perfection, and now he had been reduced to marrying a twenty-year-old ragamuffin, whose only claim to beauty was widely-spaced blue eyes and long, dark lashes. Her hair she counted one of her many minus-items.

'She was perfect, my cousin,' Sir Peter broke into her thoughts. 'As perfect—and as hard and cold as any diamond,' he went on, and Pip's eyes flickered.

They stared at each other, Pip's mind in a whirl. 'The best day's work Hallam has done is to marry you, my dear,' he went on, to her astonishment. 'You will give him back something of what Patricia took away. Take care of him.'

With another fatherly pat, he strolled away, taking the photograph with him.

Stricken with guilt because she had intended making her husband's life a misery, Pip glanced up and met the cold, venomous eyes of Vanessa Clifton. Vanessa had to be invited because her uncle was a colleague of Hallam's. At least, that was the excuse he had made. Pip wondered at the time.

Surely the niece of a colleague wasn't so important? No, Hallam invited her because he wanted to. He wanted Vanessa near him, he still cared for her. Maybe the attraction was purely physical but it was still there, and Pip could be hurt by it.

She glanced away and down at her tightly-laced fingers. She felt, rather than saw, Vanessa head in her direction and tensed herself for the confrontation. But her new husband headed Vanessa away, and Pip watched them laughing together.

My cup runneth over, Pip said to herself. He still wants her as a mistress. My job is to keep the domestic and professional side running smoothly. It was poor compensation that it would be only for a year.

She and Hallam had, on the surface, patched up their differences since that awful night Melanie left. As some kind of inducement he told Pip he had no objection to her resuming her nursing career after about a year, if she could get a place.

That, at least, was something to be grateful for. She would try to train at the local hospital, and live at White Gables. She didn't suppose for a moment he would allow her to live-in at the hospital. She would not be so readily available for her domestic and clinic chores then.

He had assured her that when Jessie Farrell retired he would try, after all, to get a replacement. In the meantime, Pip must do her best to cope. He had even offered her tuition in some of her nursing subjects so that she would have a head-start once she re-commenced training.

Eagerly she had accepted. Her very eagerness brought a strange light to his eyes, she recalled, and the storm-grey eyes had strayed to her hair, which she'd taken to wearing down these days. The sunrise hair, he'd once called it.

It was up now, though elegantly re-styled at a West End salon. She wore makeup, too, the eye-shadow emphasising her lovely eyes. At least she was presentable at the moment, and Hallam couldn't be *that* ashamed of her, could he?

The subject of her thoughts loomed over her. Vanessa was nowhere in sight and, tremulously, Pip smiled up at her husband, then the smile faded. Hallam's face was withdrawn, the eyes blank. He extended an arm courteously, and the bride and groom circulated among their guests, many of whom were beginning to drift away. The housekeeper and Sister Farrell would entertain those who remained, while the bridal pair enjoyed a long weekend in London.

If 'enjoyed' was the right word, Pip cried to herself, as she hurriedly changed into a neat, unobtrusive blue linen suit.

They slipped away, unseen by their guests. Hallam had borrowed a friend's Escort for the weekend. That, too, was blue, neat and unobtrusive. Just like me. Pip's small fists clenched and unclenched on the journey, unnoticed by her husband, who had heavy traffic to contend with.

They seemed to be a long time getting to the hotel, and Pip shot her husband a worried glance. Was the honeymoon of so little importance to him that he had forgotten they were going to London? Her anxious gaze swept this way and that, until they came to a part of London she recognised. The noise hit her, making her slight headache worse, as she leaned back and tried to relax.

Then Hallam turned into a quieter road, swept through a driveway and pulled up outside an impressive old house.

Questions trembled on Pip's lips, but the surgeon forestalled her. 'This is the private clinic where I operate. There's a patient I'm not too happy about and I thought I'd take a quick look. Shan't be long,' he added, as Pip made to follow him.

Rebuffed, she settled back, feeling grumpy. Why couldn't she go in with him? She did *so* want to see inside the clinic. It was bigger than she expected, on three floors. The driveway was tarmacked and there were a great many cars parked there.

She craned her neck, trying to see the upper floors better, and saw a nurse look briefly out of one of the windows. A nurse! Pip sighed, miserably. She *must* see inside, she must! It was so long since she'd been a nurse, so long since she'd hurried along the corridors, cared for patients, been part of the hospital family. She *would* go in! Hallam couldn't stop her. He might be ages in there if the patient wasn't responding satisfactorily.

No sooner said than done. Pip got out, re-membering to lock the door after her, then, mentally bracing herself, hurried up to the en-trance, through the swing doors, then stopped, eyes round with amazement.

It was like a palace! Of course, she had never been inside a palace, but she had her preconceived notions of what the interior would be like, the same as anyone else.

Thick, really thick, deep blue carpeting stretched over to the central reception area. To one side were elegant settees and armchairs, even a television. Nervously, she approached the reception desk, where a friendly-looking black nurse beamed at her.

Pip licked dry lips, not knowing what to say. She didn't even know which patient Hallam was visiting!

Feeling foolish, she stammered: 'Mr ... Mr Hallam Fielding. The s ... surgeon. He came in here and ... Could I wait for him?' she finished, lamely.

'Why, of course! Did you want to go up to the ward, madam?' The nurse eyed her curiously, and Pip blushed, then nodded. Why not? Why shouldn't she go up? Hallam would be cross with her in any case, so she would take the opportunity of seeing as much as she could.

A smiling porter escorted Pip to the lift, and some of her new-found determination evaporated. Hallam wouldn't just be cross, he would be furious! She closed her eyes in horror. Hallam's temper wasn't something to be induced lightly. She almost made up her mind to go down again, then the lift stopped. Mr Fielding was, the nurse had informed her, on Hamilton Ward.

So, Hamilton Ward it would be! Ahead of her stretched a long corridor. At the end of it was Hamilton Ward. Half-frightened, Pip paused at the swing-doors. Should she or shouldn't she? Yes, she would!

Firmly, she pushed open the doors and headed for Sister's office. She didn't see the rows of beds she had expected. Presumably each patient had a single room.

The office door was ajar and to Pip's relief, was occupied only by the Ward Sister, a grey-haired woman busily writing notes. She saw Pip at once, and rose.

'May I help you?'

Taking courage, Pip went right into the office. Sister seemed pleasant enough. Surely she would understand? 'I . . . I'm waiting for Hallam Fielding, the consultant surgeon. I used to do nursing and I wondered if I might wait here for him?'

'Oh, yes. Yes, naturally.' Sister looked and sounded surprised. As well she might, Pip reflected. 'Do sit down. He's with one of his patients at the moment.' Sister gestured vaguely towards a comfortable looking chair and Pip sank down, her legs suddenly weak. What would Hallam say?

Sister resumed her seat behind the desk, then glanced curiously at Pip. 'Are you a friend of Mr Fielding's?'

Pip went cold. What should she say? Oh, no, Sister. I'm his new wife! It occurred to her that he might not have told the clinic staff about his marriage. He would want to hide the fact from as many people as possible.

Pip hesitated, then opened her mouth to speak, hoping she would be forgiven a small lie, but a nurse came bustling in and Sister's attention was diverted.

Hallam was ages. It was just as well I came in, Pip decided. I would have been cold and lonely out there.

The nurse disappeared, and Sister smiled warmly at Pip. 'There, now. I've written the notes so Mr Fielding has the complete picture.' She leaned forward. 'What sort of nursing did you do?'

She sounded genuinely interested, and Pip found herself telling the woman about her few months as a student and about leaving to nurse a relative. 'I hope to go back in about a year,' Pip confided, and Sister raised a brow.

'It isn't that easy now, you know. Educational standards have risen. There are too many applicants chasing too few jobs. Hospitals can afford to pick and choose.'

Pip nodded, humbly aware of her own lack of qualifications. Six Ordinary levels was reasonable, but nothing special. She ought to have stayed on at school.

A discussion of Pip's nursing led naturally into surgery since Pip had enjoyed what little she had done of surgical nursing.

'What sort of condition do you see most?' Pip wanted to know.

'We do a lot of elective surgery. The so-called "cold cases", but we have a cardiac department as well. Mr Fielding is mainly concerned with abdominal surgery, things like ulcers, appendix, hernia, and so on.'

Pip leaned forward, eager to know more, then a frisson of fear ran along her spine and she knew, without turning, that her husband had entered the room. Now for retribution!

Both Pip and Sister rose at the same time, and Pip anxiously flicked a glance at her husband. The smile on his hard mouth was polite and intended solely for the ward Sister. Beyond a courteous nod, he ignored Pip, who stood miserably while Hallam and Sister talked shop.

Then it was over, and Pip found herself outside the ward, heading towards the lift, her husband's steely fingers fastened around her arm just above the elbow. It hurt but Pip made no complaint. No doubt there was more to come.

In silence they walked out to the car. Hallam started the engine and moved out into the traffic. This cold, condemning silence was worse than a heated argument, Pip thought.

'I'm sorry,' she said, softly. She didn't see why she should apologise but probably he expected it of her.

'Sorry?' he echoed, his eyes still on the road.

'About going into the clinic, I mean. I didn't want to embarrass you,' she went on, forlornly.

His voice was icy as he commented: 'You should have stayed where you were then, shouldn't you? What Sister Cartwright must have thought . . .' His voice trailed off, and Pip hastened to reassure him.

'I didn't tell her! I mean, she asked if I was a friend and I couldn't tell her because a nurse came in and . . . and she forgot what she'd asked me.'

The surgeon digested this information in silence, while Pip waited. Why did she always do the wrong thing?

'It is probably as well,' he agreed at last, and Pip let out an audible sigh, causing Hallam to glance sharply at her.

Then they were at their honeymoon hotel. Pip was expecting two rooms, with perhaps a bathroom, but was overjoyed to find that a whole suite was booked for them. Like a two-year-old she ran from room to room, inspecting every stick of furniture, exclaiming over the double beds in the main bedroom, the elegant white and gold furniture, the shell-pink bathroom.

The sitting-room was small and cosy, with a view over the now mist-shrouded park. They had a radio, telephone, colour television, plus a small fridge. Hallam assured her that room service would provide anything she needed, no matter at what hour of the day or night. She need not venture into the public rooms if she didn't care to. Meals could be brought up to their suite.

To Pip, this was the height of luxury. Imagine, meals delivered! Even morning tea in bed! She could stay in bed all weekend if she wished. It didn't seem right to have so much money on tap, but she supposed she would get used to it.

The only item room service could not provide was a loving husband, though. And that was something Pip desired above all else. Sir Peter's straight talking had set her right, helped put her position in perspective. She *would* give Hallam everything Patricia had not. Even herself, if he wanted her. Let him keep Vanessa on a string like an empty-headed puppet. She, Pip, had Hallam's name, his home and his protection. She would make sure he did not regret his rash proposal.

Reluctantly, Hallam agreed to her request that they dine downstairs that evening, their first together as a couple.

Determined to make him proud of her, she took extra care with her face and hair, finally deciding to wear her hair loose. She brushed the gleaming red-gold tresses until the gold glinted in the light. Despite her hatred of the colour, she was pleased with the new style. She would no longer have to plait it. The slightly shorter length just touched her shoulders, and curved under attractively.

The dress was new, for Hallam had insisted she must have some new clothes, suitable for the wife of a consultant. She had chosen carefully, not wanting him to accuse her of wasting his money.

She was parading in front of the mirror in the master bedroom when Hallam entered, after a perfunctory tap.

Bright-eyed, she turned and curtsied to him, the very full skirt of the turquoise dress billowing around her.

He seemed unable to enter into her spirit of fun, and even looked faintly embarrassed. Or was it anger that brought the dull redness to his cheeks?

Upset but unwilling to let him see, she smiled even more brightly, and went back to the dressing-table for the small pearl earrings he had given her as a wedding present. There was a brooch to match but that was for daytime wear.

Her gift to him had been a leather wallet. Very unoriginal but he had everything. Probably had several leather wallets, as well.

'If you are ready, Pip.' He sounded irritable.

She swung back to face him, the delicate gold tracery on her bodice lending her a fairytale-princess air.

'You look like a sylph, Pip,' he said, bleakly. He made no move towards her, his hands hanging limply at his side.

Out of the corner of her eye, she saw that his delicate surgeon's hands were clenched. 'Or a houri, perhaps?' she suggested, provocatively, swinging her hips gently as she glided towards him.

Roughly, he took her by the shoulders and shook her. 'For pity's sake, stop it, Pip! What are you trying to prove?' His tone was cold, but there was anguish in his stormy eyes, and something more. Was it desire?

Pip didn't know, hadn't the experience to help her. All she knew was that she loved him. He would never love her but if she could somehow make him want her, wouldn't that be sufficient?

She put her small hands on his chest and gazed up at him, putting her whole heart into her searching gaze. 'Please don't be angry, Hallam. I just w . . . want to make you happy.'

'Happy?' he repeated. 'I can never be happy with you, Pip. Never. I'll wait outside.' With one swift movement he was gone, and Pip stared at the closed door.

He had shut the door in her face in more ways than one. *I can never be happy with you.* He had actually come out into the open and admitted it.

He didn't expect her to bring him happiness. He didn't love her, and often she felt he did not even *like* her.

Was it Melanie he yearned for? Or Vanessa? Pip didn't know, and her poor heart was breaking. Here she was, a married woman, a bride on her wedding night, and she didn't know which woman her husband loved. One thing for sure—he did not love his new wife.

Afterwards, she remembered nothing of the meal, except that he let her choose her own food. It might have been plastic she ate, or bits of wood. Whatever it was, the food was wasted on her. Her mind darted this way and that, seeking a solution to her problem.

She smiled wryly. Her wedding day and already she had a marital problem!

'Something amusing you, Pip?' her husband asked softly, and she cast him a quick glance. He looked concerned, tender, even. Concerned because he felt guilty at marrying her, all the while believing she cared for his brother.

That was it! She would taunt him about Geoff, make him jealous. He would be so infuriated that— that, what? She bit her lip anxiously. Just what *would* he do? Hit her? No, he wasn't the type. Make passionate love to her? Her cheeks burned. Indeed, she felt the heat covering her whole body. Of course he wouldn't make love to her. Why should he? He wanted Vanessa Clifton. Or Melanie. Which was it?

She caught his eye and smiled at him, but he was far from pleased and stared at her, the firm mouth set in its inevitable hard line, the harsh planes of his face becoming a formidable mask.

If only she could get through to him! Find out what made him tick. There must be a key somewhere. If only . . .

'You're having quite an argument with yourself, Pip,' he said, blandly.

'Oh! I didn't know it was so obvious,' she muttered, miserable because she wanted to fling her arms around him and could not.

'Time to go up, I think,' he announced, getting to his feet and helping her up. Her heart fluttered. Time for bed.

'You've had a tiring day, Pip. Try to get some sleep, there's a good girl.' He gave her shoulder an avuncular pat and she flinched.

Good girl, indeed! I'm your wife! she wanted to scream. *I love you! I don't want to be a good girl!*

He made some sound when she flinched away but she was unable to catch any words. Not waiting to see if he would follow, she hurried towards the lift, her only desire to get as far away from him as possible. She meant nothing to him, nothing! She didn't think her heart could take any more sorrow, not just yet.

She was alone in the lift, except for the lift-boy, and dismay fought with relief that he wasn't coming to bed. It was early for him. Probably he would take a stroll, or have a nightcap in the bar.

Pip was tempted to go all the way down again, to see if she could find him, then rejected the idea. She would appear foolish in his eyes, more foolish than she did already.

Back in their suite, she paced up and down a few times, unable to settle to anything. Why didn't he come? Was he expecting her to go straight to bed? Was he waiting until she did, before turning in himself?

Eventually, she decided she would take a leisurely bath. She cleaned off all her new make-up, washed her face with soap and water, then glanced at her reflection. A freshly-scrubbed teenage face, glowing with health, stared back at her. She could have been any fifteen-year-old. *But I'm not fifteen!* she wailed. *I'm Mrs Philippa Fielding, a married woman!*

The virgin bride, she thought crossly, then stepped into the luxurious sunken bath and soaked away her sorrows.

Her trousseau nightdress was white lace over deep peach satin and had been terribly expensive. But at least she'd bought it with her own money. Hallam told her she would receive a monthly allowance to spend just as she wished. In lieu of salary, she supposed. She was working out cheap as he would not now have to pay her a salary. On that basis she decided she was well worth the monthly pocket-money and fully intended to put it to good use. How lovely to have money of her own, to spend on herself for a change.

He had given her a handsome cheque to pay for her trousseau and any little items she needed, but she had been sparing with that, and intended returning what she had left.

With a little troubled sigh, she got out and rubbed herself down on one of several soft pink towels. Money to pay for a glamorous trousseau—and no groom to see her in all her finery!

Tears pricked her eyelids. She must not cry, her face would get all red and blotchy. But Hallam wouldn't see it, anyway, so I'll have a good cry, she muttered, the hot tears cascading down her thin face as she stepped into the beautiful lacy nightgown. What did it matter what she looked like? Nothing mattered any more.

Hallam did not love her. He told her to her face that she could never make him happy. There was no point in keeping up the pretence. She loved and he was indifferent. And it hurt! Oh, how it hurt. The pain was almost physical.

She curled up on the deep pink pile carpet of her bedroom. She didn't know why she did it, but she left the door of her room slightly ajar. Of course there was no possibility of him coming in to wish her goodnight. Was there? No, he would go straight to his bedroom, the small dressing-room adjoining hers which he'd taken for his own.

She could weep all night and he wouldn't hear. Would never know her sorrow. She hated him! Wildly, she kicked her legs in a futile display of temper, before once more trying to bury her head in the carpet as a fresh bout of weeping overtook her.

A far-from-gentle hand shook her, but angrily she pulled away. Whoever it was, she wasn't interested.

Then she was hauled roughly to her feet and given a good shaking. Hallam towered above her, face distorted by rage.

'Stop it!' she wailed, trying to fight him off. 'Stop, please!' she begged, waiting for him to stop so she could hit him. He wasn't going to treat her that way!

But her husband seemed to lose control for a few moments and continued shaking her until her poor head ached. She was no longer really crying but her breath was coming in great gulping sobs, and she had to fight just to breathe. *'Please!'*

He swore, and abruptly pushed her from him. Pip staggered but didn't fall. It took her a few seconds to regain her breath, then, wild-eyed, she lunged at him, hitting out at every part of his body she could reach.

She would not be treated like that! She would not!

Strong arms gathered her in and she was unable to move, imprisoned as she was against his chest. He had removed his jacket, and through the thin shirt she could feel the pounding of his heart. The warmth of his body percolated through to her and she sighed, snuggling as close to his chest as she could. This was heaven!

'I didn't meant to shake you, Pip, but you make me so angry!' he murmured against her hair.

'You make me angry, too!' she said, pertly, and was overjoyed to hear him chuckle.

'We're bad for each other, Pip,' he said, holding her away from him, and her smile faded.

Rejection again. 'If the mountain won't come to Mohammed then Mohammed must come to the mountain,' she intoned softly, devouring him with her big blue eyes. Greatly daring, and past caring what he thought of her flighty ways, she put her arms around his waist and snuggled up to his body again. Closing her eyes, she waited, fully prepared to find herself tossed across the room in Hallam's fury. But she wasn't prepared for his embrace, the tightening of his arms about her, the shudder that swept through him, communicating his urgency to Pip.

Afraid now of what she had invoked, she struggled to free herself, but it was too late. He picked her up as though she weighed no more than a feather, and threw her onto one of the double beds.

Panic-stricken, she tried to roll off but he was too quick. His lean body was on hers, his weight pinning her very effectively to the bed.

'Weren't you warned not to play with fire, Pip?' he asked hoarsely. His face was only inches from hers and she gazed lovingly into those dark, storm-grey eyes, all the fight gone from her. The warmth of his body was heating her. It was a delicious feeling, and her eyes half closed waiting for his kiss, hoping he wouldn't send her away in disgust. Unconsciously, her lips parted and when his hard mouth came down on hers, she responded passionately.

He seemed content just to kiss her, but she wasn't. Her fevered body tingled with desire for him. She belonged to Hallam. Didn't he want her?

The kisses were awakening her, as though she was Sleeping Beauty coming back to this world after her long sleep. She began to lick Hallam's dear face, then turned her head away, teasingly, and his mouth found her ear instead. Gently, he nibbled it and she squirmed with pleasure.

'Hallam,' she whispered, then felt the bed shake as he got up. The enveloping warmth that was his body left her, and she shivered. He sat up, not touching her, eyes sombre.

'Forgive me, Pip. I had no right,' he said brokenly, and her eyes flashed.

'Right! Who has more right than you!' she snapped, very near to tears again. 'W . . . what was the point in marrying me if you . . . you don't want me?' she finished lamely, eyes downcast.

'I married you for your own good, my dear,' he said, softly. She stared at him with distrust.

'It's true,' he insisted, his long fingers gently caressing her bare arm. 'I think I've always cared for you,' he went on, to her astonishment. 'That first day, at the interview, you spoke up for yourself. You weren't going to be brow-beaten by any stuffy old surgeon!'

Impishly, she fluttered her long lashes at him. 'You *were* stuffy!' she insisted, laughing.

White teeth gleamed as he joined in the laughter. 'I believe I was!' He added softly: 'I hope you will become as fond of me as I am of you, Pip.'

Her eyes lit up, but he spoiled it. 'I always wanted a daughter. Now I have one. Thank you, my dear.'

Shocked, Pip sat up, unaware how much of her body she was showing.

With one of his rapid mood swings he got up and said in a carefully-controlled voice: 'Get a good night's sleep. We can talk in the morning.' He made a movement towards the door, but she was on her feet.

'No! I won't let you go!' Feverishly she searched for some way of keeping him with her, some tactical weapon she could use. Then it came to her. 'Geoffrey wouldn't leave me to spend my wedding night alone!' she said, and Hallam's tightly leashed control exploded into fury.

'Geoffrey! Will you get him out of your mind!' he snarled. 'Never speak about him in that way again!'

Frightened by his outburst, she ground out:

'He's a man! *He* wouldn't pretend I was a substitute daughter! I don't suppose *he* lives like a monk!'

Hallam's face became a cold, impassive mask as he moved towards her. Fearing he would beat her, she shrank back but there was to be no escape. Somehow, she found herself on the bed again, and lay there breathing hard, watching Hallam through half-closed lids as he rapidly undressed. She'd won the fight, but at what cost?

Wondering how much pain there would be, she began to shake as though in a fever. Yet her limbs were incapable of movement. Her nightgown, the lovely lacy creation, was just as rapidly removed and now she really was terrified. She must stop him!

'Hallam, I didn't . . .' she began, then his kisses melted her resistance, and her skin tingled with anticipation as those long, delicate fingers caressed her. His hands moved searchingly, probingly, over her body, and she almost squealed with pleasure. She didn't think there could be any more delights in store, then she did cry out as his touch became more intimate, and the pressure of his thighs increased, bearing her into a land of pleasure and rapture.

It was morning when she awoke, aching delightfully all over. For a moment she wondered why the bed was an unfamiliar one. Then it all came back, and she closed her eyes again, sighing a little as she recalled each intimate, loving moment she had spent in her husband's arms. He loved her! He must do, surely? It didn't matter, she was far too sated to puzzle it out now. Such intellectual exercise must wait. Whether he truly loved her or merely desired her body, it made no difference to her feelings for him.

'Pip.' A cold voice spoke nearby, and, resentfully, she pulled herself awake, then her lips curved into a smile, as she saw Hallam sitting by the bed.

He was fully clothed now and looked as if he might have sat there all night if she hadn't known better. 'I owe you an apology, Pip,' he began. When her lips parted to protest, he waved her down.

'I did not intend that to happen. It was largely your own fault for taunting me about Geoffrey. But I should have had more control. I lost that control, you drove me half out of my mind and I'm not proud of it.' She listened, horrified, as the cold, precise voice continued: 'We will return to White Gables straight away, after breakfast. It will give you a chance to settle in before my next clinic on Monday. This ...' Here he waved a hand vaguely at her still naked form, 'this episode will not be repeated. I can't say how sorry I am but I will make it up to you, somehow.'

He sounded desperately tired, but for once Pip didn't care. 'How can you make it up to me?' she demanded. 'You can't replace what you've taken!' she went on, trying to hurt him, and succeeding, for he stood up, anguish all over his face.

'Oh, Hallam! I'm sorry,' she wailed, getting out of bed, intent only on comforting him, then realised she had nothing on. Her face and body went as red as her hair as she hurriedly dived between the sheets again.

She buried her head under the pillow, and when she emerged, Hallam was gone. Burning with shame and embarrassment, she bathed and dressed,

then packed the few items she'd brought with her.
The honeymoon was over. Hallam said it was a
mistake, a brief loss of control that would not
occur again. He not only didn't love her, he obviously didn't even desire her. He thought of her as
a child. She had made the running, she was the
one who had enticed him to bed. She was a shame-
less hussy. She'd taken his pride, his self-respect
away. Had she destroyed him altogether? He was,
underneath the harsh exterior, a shy, diffident man.
She had no right to taunt him about Geoffrey. She
was the one who ought to apologise, to assure him
she would keep her distance in the future, and she
would do it right now.

He wasn't in their suite and she presumed he
had gone down to breakfast. She would join him
there, let him see she could behave in a civilized
manner. She would not embarrass him again.

Her mind made up, she ran lightly down the
stairs, scorning the lift. Head held proudly, she
walked into the dining-room, and made straight
for their table.

Too late she saw that he wasn't alone. There
was no mistaking the tiny brunette who was laughing up at him. Vanessa! Even on his honeymoon,
he wouldn't do without that woman. Hurt and
bitter, she was about to retreat, but it was too late.
Hallam's grey eyes were on her, her own shock
mirrored in his. He half-rose, then Vanessa saw
her.

'Do come and join us, Pip! I'm just enjoying a
late breakfast! Hearing all the news, you might
say!' Vanessa went on, her tone light but the green
eyes vindictive.

With great dignity, Pip smiled at them both. Yes,

why not join them? After breakfast Hallam could make love to Vanessa Clifton. Variety was the spice of life.

CHAPTER SEVEN

HALLAM was speechless but quickly recovered and beckoned a waiter to bring another chair, letting Pip have his chair in the meantime.

Pip sat down and smiled innocently at Vanessa, whose eyes narrowed thoughtfully. 'Are you staying here, too?' Pip asked, with an air of genuine interest, and Vanessa nodded.

'It's such a coincidence!' Vanessa trilled, shooting a coy glance at the surgeon. 'I had no idea ... Naturally I wouldn't have disturbed your ... honeymoon for the world!'

Pip continued to smile. No-one would ever know what it cost. The slight hesitation before Vanessa used the word 'honeymoon' wasn't lost on her. Had Hallam assured his mistress that his marriage would be in name only? Was Vanessa expecting Hallam to be in the mood for love-making later in the day?

Well, hard luck, Vanessa! Pip thought, daringly laying her small, well-kept hand on Hallam's sleeve. She wasn't blind to the hate-filled look the other girl directed at her. Only, of course, Vanessa smiled at the same time so that Hallam should think she and Pip were the best of friends.

Pip adamantly refused to move her hand and, to her surprise, Hallam made no attempt to dislodge it. She had to, when the breakfast arrived, but contented herself with casting longing looks at him, or gently giggling to herself and smiling at her hus-

114

band, as though they shared a private joke.

The atmosphere grew tense. Hallam seemed to have lost his appetite and ate only toast and marmalade with two cups of coffee. Pip, too, had no appetite, and longed for Vanessa to leave them in peace. She had something important to say to her new husband!

The meal could not be prolonged, and both girls reached for Hallam's arm as they left the table. Laughing shakily, Vanessa removed hers, but Pip held on grimly. She wasn't letting him out of her sight. Not while Little Miss Predator was around!

Head held high, Pip walked determinedly away from Vanessa, almost pulling Hallam over in her hurry to get away. She didn't relax until they were in the lift. She would have preferred the stairs but the lift was open, invitingly, and they must get away.

Hallam gave her a quizzical look but made no comment until they were back in their suite. Only then did Pip relax. Her hands were trembly and blue, and with a quick gesture Hallam took hold of them, making her stretch her arms out in front of her.

Questions trembled on Pip's lips, but he let go of her and stood back, watching. 'Hm. One of the signs of Raynaud's disease.'

'Whose disease?' Pip didn't much care but if she had a disease she felt she ought to know its name.

'Raynaud's. Coldness of extremities, generally hands and fingers. They go blue, sometimes purple.'

'Oh.' And she had foolishly believed he'd caught hold of her hands because he *wanted* to touch her! Foolish girl. No doubt he would be quite pleased if she had some obscure disease. He had such a clinical mind he could discuss it with her on the journey home!

Well, she *did* have a disease. She was suffering from an allergic reaction to Vanessa Clifton! 'Odd meeting Vanessa here, wasn't it?' she said mildly, packing away the undies she had only recently unpacked.

But Hallam wouldn't be drawn. 'She enjoys a weekend in London. Goes to the theatre a lot, I believe.'

Pip bit her tongue until it hurt. She knew very well Vanessa was fond of theatre-going. *And* she knew who generally escorted her. 'It's a pity our stay is so brief,' she went on, conversationally, hesitantly packing her new nightie on top. 'We could have gone to the theatre with her.'

'She isn't staying. I've offered her a lift back.'

Pip swung round, horrified. 'No, you wouldn't do that to me,' she whispered. 'You couldn't.'

'Do what, Pip?' He sounded annoyed, his face setting into the harsh lines she knew so well. 'The girl hasn't any transport. Her car broke down. The least I could do was to offer her a lift, surely?'

'Honemoon for three,' Pip said bitterly, as though he hadn't spoken.

'For God's sake, Pip! Act your age! Anyone would think you were jealous of poor Vanessa.'

'Poor Vanessa,' Pip echoed, unable to hide her fury any longer. 'What about poor Pip—sharing her honeymoon and her husband with the other woman!'

Hallam ignored the remark. 'Poor Vanessa was embarrassed and actually refused a lift. Said she knew she would be in the way. Of course, I assured her you would make her welcome. You *will* make her welcome, Pip,' he carried on, sternly. 'She and her uncle have been friends of mine for a very long time. I will not have them slighted. Do you hear?' He moved closer, and Pip nodded numbly, then hurried out to the bathroom so that Hallam should not see the tears she could no longer keep back.

'This patient should interest you, Pip.'

Pip's sad eyes met her husband's. 'Yes?'

'Mm. She's probably got Raynaud's disease, though there is a differential diagnosis.'

'Oh?' Pip spoke politely, well remembering the day Hallam decided *she* had one of the symptoms! Nearly a week had passed now, and Pip was settling down to her duties. In fact, her duties were little different from those as a secretary-companion. They did not include keeping the surgeon warm at night.

Try as she might, Pip couldn't put from her that one poignant memory, her wedding night, the hours she had spent warm and comfortable in her husband's arms. As the years went by, she mused glumly, the memory would fade a little. Indeed, when she was middle-aged she might believe it had all been an erotic dream, wishful thinking on her part. She didn't *feel* any different. She'd imagined being made love to altered one's personality, showed in some way, but it didn't appear to. Aunt Norah hadn't commented on her appearance so Pip decided the wedding night had left no visible mark.

But, oh, she loved him! *How* she loved him! And the hateful man didn't care one jot for her. All he wanted was Vanessa Clifton—perhaps because she was experienced in that sort of thing.

'I beg your pardon?' Pip became aware that Hallam was staring at her. Self-consciously, she fiddled with a curl, then watched, fascinated, as the gesture brought dull colour to Hallam's cheeks. There must be something about her hair that bothered him. She would have to put it up again.

'I asked what you knew about Raynaud's disease,' he said testily.

He was glaring now, as though he positively disliked her! She bit her lip, willing herself not to cry. She was becoming distressingly emotional since discovering she loved him.

She racked her brains, but no glimmer of light showed. What was it about Raynaud's syndrome? Ah. 'Their hands are very cold, sometimes trembly,' she intoned, just as if she was airing her knowledge in front of the examiner. 'When their fingers are cold they become very pale, then blue. Sometimes after that they go red. Rather pretty,' she added, just to annoy him.

'And the surgical treatment?' Hallam did not rise to the bait and Pip was disappointed. If, once, they had a really good quarrel, they might end up in each other's arms! It was a forlorn hope. But anything would be better than this cold, courteous indifference. She might well be a casual acquaintance instead of his wife.

'I'll bet you don't treat Vanessa like this!' she exploded, much to her husband's astonishment.

'Like what? She isn't a nurse, and I wouldn't expect her to know about these conditions, Pip. You *are* an extraordinary girl!' he went on, shaking his head sadly as though she was a hopeless case.

'I am *not*!' Pip cried. 'But I ... I d ... don't

know any more about Raynaud's disease. Nor, frankly, do I care!' She stared at him wildly, feeling as though she could hit him. She *would* hit him!

No sooner the thought than the act. Pip picked up a glazed vase her husband was particularly fond of, and hurled it at him. Fortunately, perhaps, her aim was awry and the vase splintered harmlessly against the wall.

Far from arousing Hallam's anger so that they could have a blazing row, he appeared only mildly interested. For a moment he stared at the fragments. 'Didn't you like that vase, Pip?' he asked, clearly not at all bothered that she might have injured him.

'I . . . I,' Pip began, but couldn't find words. How on earth could you quarrel with someone like that? His normally explosive temper seemed to have gone on holiday.

Weakly, Pip sat down again at her desk. They were in the office at White Gables and there was masses of correspondence to be attended to. She had three sets of case-notes to type, and she just could not find the energy. She was mentally rather than physically tired. She couldn't relax for a second without all sorts of gloomy pictures crowding into her mind—Hallam kissing Vanessa, the two of them breakfasting together or at the theatre. Although she didn't believe Hallam would be blatant about his affair with Vanessa, he had been out on two evenings since their return and had come home quite late. Both absences had been unexplained, her husband merely stating that he had a pressing engagement.

I'll just bet she was pressing! Pip thought fiercely. She hated them both. She wished she had never set eyes on the hateful man! Never fallen in love with him, never enticed him to bed ... Well, no, she mused, feeling the swift tide of colour, she didn't regret that!

'I've made arrangements for you to help out at the clinic once a week, Pip.' Hallam's precise voice broke into her thoughts, and she blushed more.

'Oh?'

'Now that Aunt Norah has left, it occurred to me that you won't have enough work to occupy you.'

Pip opened her mouth in ready denial, but the surgeon went on, relentlessly: 'You can't say you are overworked or unduly tired, can you? That extraordinary display of temper wasn't the act of a weary woman. The vase was heavy and it took considerable strength to throw it that far,' he went on calmly.

'You ... you ... you skunk!' she finally managed.

'I bath regularly,' he commented, one corner of his mouth turning up in amusement.

'I didn't mean that. You know perfectly well what I meant.'

He gave an exasperated sigh, the unexpected good humour leaving him. 'I doubt that even you know what you mean, Pip. I thought I had married a woman, but you're just a child! Can't you grow up a little? Make some effort?'

Hallam moved towards the desk, and Pip held her breath. Oh, Hallam, please be kind, she thought. Please tell me you care.

But he didn't. He merely patted her head as though she was the little child he'd called her, then just as quickly withdrew his hand as though he regretted the gesture the minute it was made.

He couldn't bear her near him. He couldn't bear to touch, or even look at her. It was so obvious and it hurt. Sometimes Pip felt she could not take it one more hour. It was a nagging pain which never quite left her, a gnawing away at her heart, at her confidence.

Why, since he thought so little of her, he had bothered to marry her, Pip didn't know. It must be as he had said—that he must think of his reputation, and that it would be so useful to have a wife-cum-secretary at his beck and call night and day. No, she corrected herself, wryly, day not night. Vanessa was for nights, or at least evenings.

Perhaps, in some way, Pip *was* the daughter he had longed for. Certainly he was a lonely man, a man who needed the warmth and attention of family life.

She settled back to her work, Hallam having gone through to his consulting-room. It was going to be a very long year. In fact, she wasn't sure she could last that long. Hallam was so near yet so far from her. She did so long to touch him. Her fingers itched to loosen his tie when he came back from his visits, or to smooth back that lock of straight black hair which had an endearing habit of falling over his left eye!

Yet, she had made the running once and regretted it ever since. She couldn't do it again. Could she? Dare she?

Yes, why not! She would start this evening, before her courage deserted her.

Her excitement bubbling over, Pip had difficulty concentrating on her work. But somehow she kept her face impassive, her voice normal, so that when

Hallam brought in some more notes to be typed, she was able to converse with him normally. The angry little scene might never have been. Pip was once again the reasonably efficient secretary-cum-dogsbody and Hallam finally went off to call at the clinic, blissfully unaware that Pip intended seducing him.

Hallam would be back late for dinner, Pip knew, but the office work left her little time to prepare herself. The housekeeper, Mrs Hutchins, still provided their evening meal, preparing it in advance, and this evening there was chicken with herbs, mushrooms and tomatoes, with a cold sweet to follow. The meal would be cooked by the time Hallam returned, and there was little Pip need do other than lay the table.

She allowed herself the luxury of a leisurely bath, shaking in nearly half a packet of bath crystals. Afterwards, she dabbed a little scent behind each ear and on her pulse-spots. It was Panache, the perfume which Vanessa Clifton used. Obviously the surgeon liked it!

What to wear presented no problem. Whatever his faults Hallam was generous to her and gave her a far bigger allowance than she thought necessary. She knew what it was like wondering where your next penny was coming from, so, like a little squirrel, she had salted some of it away in a building society. The proverbial rainy day might come at any time. But some she spent on clothes, and now she lifted out her favourite dress, one that Hallam had not yet seen. It was a deep, vibrant green, not a bright green but rather a series of different shades, the palest leaf green gradually merging into emerald. It was mid-calf length, filmy, with what seemed to Pip to be a disgustingly low neckline. If that didn't set her husband's pulses racing, nothing would.

Hallam was later than Pip expected, and she had ample time to get ready. The dress suited her, she knew, emphasising as it did her small, rounded breasts and incredibly tiny waist. She'd brushed her hair until it crackled with life, and when the light caught it, it truly resembled the sunrise that Hallam had once called it. She wore Hallam's wedding gift, the pearl earrings, but no other jewellery, since the dress itself needed no embellishment.

She wished she had a pretty dress ring, though. She rather fancied an opal she'd seen in the local jewellers but was reluctant to spend so much money on a luxury. Hallam had not thought to buy her an engagement ring, and she gazed wistfully at the plain gold ring on her left hand. Though she was proud of it, it looked lonely by itself and she decided she would save up her allowance, until she could buy a small, discreet diamond ring to go with it.

Of course, Vanessa had commented on the omission, just before the wedding. Not in Hallam's hearing, though. Vanessa had a split personality, Pip thought. It wasn't a normal bitchiness, it went far deeper. On one side was the beautiful, elegantly slim young woman who laughed a lot, who clearly adored Hallam, and was touchingly sweet to Hallam's wife. But the other Vanessa was much darker, a sour, embittered woman whose plans for the future had been crushed by the surgeon's marriage. Being merely the mistress was not good enough for Vanessa. Hallam was a wealthy man. Moreover, he was a surgeon much respected by

other members of his profession. Apart from his
National Health work, he operated at a small, ex-
clusive and world-famous clinic in London and his
services were highly sought after. He had contrib-
uted to research projects and was the author of
several monographs and a surgical textbook. The
step to a professorial post would be a small one,
Pip reflected proudly, as she sat at the long dining-
table waiting for Hallam to return. No wonder
Vanessa was put out! He was a clever, dedicated
surgeon and she was an incredibly lucky girl to be
chosen as his bride—even if it was for the wrong
reasons.

She glanced at the clock, then took a closer look.
Heavens, he *was* late. Nearly eight o'clock. Pip was
too excited, too over-wrought to eat anything, but
she decided that a drink would settle her down.

Hallam liked wine with his meals and was
something of a connoisseur, so she always left the
choice to him. To her, one wine was much the same
as another. However . . . She opened the door of
the big, highly polished cocktail cabinet and peered
inside. Hallam kept his best wines in a small cellar
but in the cabinet there was a choice of sherry,
Scotch or cognac. Yes, brandy! Good for shock.
Pip giggled. Hallam would be the one needing
treatment for shock!

She poured herself a generous amount of brandy
and tossed it back the way they did with rye whis-
key in Westerns, then wished she hadn't as the raw
spirit went down, burning and choking her as it
did so.

Gasping and red-faced, feeling her stomach was
on fire, Pip sat down on the carpet. She wasn't
sure she liked the taste and if that was what even

good brandy did, she wasn't going to repeat the experiment.

Unsteadily, she got to her feet. Her head began to swim and she realised how stupid she was to drink on an empty stomach. She reached for one of the crisp rolls Hallam liked at dinner and munched away. Now a warm glow was spreading throughout her body. She felt a little heartburn but the bread roll would soon cure that.

Pip enjoyed the feeling so much that she poured herself another brandy, being careful this time to sip it slowly. It was said that alcohol gave one courage to face the unpleasant realities of life, and she defended herself by insisting, aloud, that Hallam was so nasty that she *needed* a little extra courage. And he was so late.

Had he met with an accident? Pip sat up, horrified. The idea simply had not occurred to her before. Whenever Hallam was unexpectedly detained either at the clinic or at the local hospital he always phoned or got the ward Sister to do so. Should she ring the clinic, just in case he was still there?

Worriedly, she nibbled her lower lip. What if they said he'd left hours ago! What would she do then? If he wasn't at the clinic, where was he? With Vanessa, perhaps? a little voice muttered darkly, and she clenched her fists. No! He couldn't be!

But she knew very well he could. And if she telephoned the clinic and he wasn't there, they would know that she had a husband she couldn't keep tabs on. It would be so humiliating.

Yet she had to know. The waiting was killing her, despite the warm, cosy feeling induced by the alcohol. She would just have one more small glass, another nibble at the bread-roll, then phone. Probably he had an emergency and simply hadn't remembered Pip, waiting anxiously at home.

She felt very sleepy after her next brandy, and it was an effort to lift the telephone receiver. Then she found she could not recall the number of the clinic. The ability to remember phone numbers was one she prided herself on, and, disgruntled, she was forced to look it up in the index which Hallam kept under the telephone.

When she found the number, she stared at it for some time, but her wits had deserted her and she couldn't remember *why* she had wanted the number in the first place.

Shaking her clouded head, Pip wandered back to the warmth of the fire, sank down on to the carpet and tiredly laid her head on her arms.

She was still there when Hallam returned, only minutes later. By now Pip was curled up cosily in front of the fire, the lovely green dress wrapped around her like a shawl.

The voices gradually penetrated her clouded consciousness, and she thought she heard Hallam. Dear Hallam, he'd come home! Wearily, she closed her eyes again and tried to resist when she felt strong arms lifting her.

'She's drunk!' another voice, a female voice, said. 'Hallam, she's drunk! How *awful* for you!'

Pip opened one eye and saw the dark hairs on one of the hands that supported her. Hallam's hand. His hands were under her armpits, and she was thoroughly enjoying the sensation! Something her husband was not.

She opened both eyes and focussed on Vanessa. He'd brought Vanessa home for dinner! Pip went crimson, then hung limply, hoping Hallam would think she had fainted. Anything to get away from the awful scene. But she wasn't to escape so easily.

'Pip! Speak to me,' her husband commanded.

'I'm very tired,' Pip said weakly, then moaned as Hallam let her slide to the carpet again.

'Let *me* help her, Hallam!' Vanessa's shrill voice penetrated Pip's alcohol-induced anaesthesia, and she began to shake her head, but wished she hadn't.

Vanessa's help could not be evaded, however, and Pip found herself in Hallam's arms, being carried up to her room. She hadn't the strength to protest, and barely heard him leave the room. Sighing, she snuggled into the lacy counterpane. Alone at last.

But she wasn't. To her horror, she felt hands removing her shoes and pulling her tights down quickly. She could hardly open her eyes but she must. Surely Hallam had gone. The hands tugged viciously at the zip of her pretty dress, then jerked it off, scratching Pip's back.

The undresser swore, and Pip knew then that it was a woman. She was alone and at the mercy of Vanessa!

'Damn you! I've broken a nail,' Vanessa wailed, pushing Pip back against the cover.

'Don't. Please.' Pip protested weakly. She honestly didn't have the strength to fight Vanessa. She just wanted to be left alone, but it wasn't to be.

'You little tramp!' Vanessa hissed in her ear. She pushed her face right up against Pip's, and glared.

Pip flinched and edged away, but Vanessa's hate-filled voice followed her. 'You took Hallam away!'

she went on, with tears streaming down her cheeks, but Pip merely stared. She was incapable of emotion. The drink had done its job too well. The whole scene took on an unreal quality. Pip seemed to be floating above the stage, watching herself and Vanessa arguing. Or rather, Vanessa was arguing. She might as well have been talking to herself for all the notice Pip was able to take.

Vanessa half-choked on a sob as Pip calmly looked on, then continued: 'He *married* you, but he *loves* me! We ... we had a lovely evening until he remembered you. "I'd better get home," he said. He always comes home to you!' Vanessa wailed, and Pip began to nod understandingly, then remembered her delicate head.

'Yes, he always does,' she agreed, but this brought fresh tears to her rival's by now blotchy face.

'I hate you,' Vanessa snapped, between the tears. 'I've been Hallam's mistress for so long. He loved me. He told me so,' she continued, her voice only a whisper now. 'Yet he married *you*!' Suddenly, Vanessa lunged forward and rolled Pip on to the fortunately thickly-carpeted floor, then the door closed quietly, and a bruised Pip lay there for a long time before sleep finally claimed her.

It hardly seemed any time at all when she felt herself being shaken. She opened tired eyes, to find Hallam bending over her. 'Pip! Get up, for God's sake!'

Pip didn't think she would make it, she really was dreadfully weary, but she tried and managed to kneel. She needed her husband's assistance to stand, though.

He propped her against the wall, and Pip closed

her eyes. She recalled the events of the evening only too well now. Her pretty dress, torn off her back by a spiteful rival, the surfeit of brandy, the embarrassment of it all.

A lone tear made its way down her cheek, and Hallam leaned forward and gently brushed it away. 'Oh, Hallam, I'm so sorry!' Pip said, her blue eyes pleading for understanding. 'I wanted you to see my new dress.'

'Is this it?' He picked up the filmy dress from the end of the bed where Vanessa had flung it. 'It's very pretty, Pip. Lovely colour.'

Pip's eyes widened. He wasn't angry. The saints be praised! 'I'm glad you like it,' she murmured happily. 'Is it still Tuesday?'

Dark eyes surveyed her, noting the flushed face, the too-bright eyes. 'Yes, still Tuesday. It's nearly midnight. Hadn't you better get into bed? I thought Vanessa had put you to bed,' he went on, half to himself, his long, surgeon's fingers examining the broken zip on the dress.

'She hates me,' Pip whispered, her eyes also on the broken zip and torn dress. 'She dragged it off my back and . . . and broke the zip,' she muttered, too sad to be angry, for hadn't Vanessa said: 'I've been Hallam's mistress for so long'? Presumably she still was.

'Who broke the zip?' Hallam asked sharply.

'Vanessa. She hates me. Perhaps she loves you,' Pip said thoughtfully.

'Vanessa tore the dress?' Hallam asked, his voice cold and Pip nodded, then looked down at what remained of her clothing.

'I'll get undressed, if you don't mind,' she began, then her hair was tugged viciously, jerking her poor head back. Hallam's eyes blazed down at her.

Her lips parted but no sound emerged. 'I know you have an unreasoning dislike of Vanessa, but this is ridiculous!' Hallam stormed. 'Vanessa is a sweet girl. She fully understands why I married you,' he went on, his grip still painfully on her hair. 'She is prepared to be your friend, and this . . . *this* is how you repay her. By spreading lies, and making false accusations.'

Abruptly, the pressure on her hair ceased, and Pip put her hands over her ears, unwilling to listen to any more praise for the 'sweet-natured' Vanessa. It was incredible that such an intelligent man could be so blind!

He closed the door noisily, and Pip sat on the edge of her bed. Love was said to be blind. That must be it. Hallam loved Vanessa and Vanessa loved Hallam. For Philippa Fielding, née Weston, there was no room.

'Each patient has his own room, except for the last two rooms, nine and ten, which are four-bedded.' The matron's precise voice explained to Pip all she needed to know about the layout of the private clinic.

Hallam, true to his word, had arranged for her to spend one day a week there, easing herself in gently to the routine. And, Pip reflected bitterly, it left him one whole day to dally with Vanessa.

Her duties would be only those of an auxiliary because she had completed very little of her training when her mother's illness interrupted it. But Pip was a cheerful, willing soul, and didn't mind in the least. One day a week she would feel needed. That was the important thing. Hallam didn't need her. By his spirited defence of his mistress, he had made that perfectly clear.

CHAPTER EIGHT

DESPITE her heartache, Pip settled down well to her new routine; one full day each week at the clinic, three afternoons assisting Hallam with his private patients, plus four mornings catching up on the secretarial work. That left all day Saturday and Sunday free plus Wednesday afternoons.

Hallam's niece, Alison, moved into the flat. She would be getting married in a couple of weeks and wanted to settle in first. She was a tall, slender blonde, and bore not the slightest resemblance to the saturnine surgeon. Perhaps that was why Pip got on so well with her.

Having the weekends free should have been lovely, but Saturday and Sunday were lonely days for Pip. Alison usually spent weekends with her fiancé's people, and Hallam ... Just where did Hallam disappear to on Saturday evenings?

He spent a great deal of time shut up in his study and it was more than Pip dared to disturb him. Indeed, she felt more of an intruder than ever. Once Hallam nearly called her 'Miss Weston'. He'd forgotten their wedding night already! She was just a secretary now, a useful, hard-working member of staff. Certainly she was no longer a wife.

Monday again, a cold but bright October day. Pip never got that Monday-morning feeling and genuinely looked forward to her day at the clinic. Hallam always drove her there because he had patients to see before going on to his part-time post

at the General. She had to make her own way back
on the bus, though. Back to a warm yet curiously
cold house. White Gables welcomed her, yet the
aloof surgeon did not.

'Had a couple of new patients in during the
week,' her husband commented, as the car turned
into the clinic entrance.

'Oh. Who?'

'Sir David—ulcer. And Mrs Watts.'

'Oh, that nice, dumpy little woman?'

What might have been the ghost of a smile flickered across his lean face, but Pip may have
imagined it. 'She *is* a nice little woman,' he agreed,
as he locked the car and motioned for her to
proceed him through the swing doors of the clinic.
'She has a troublesome gall-bladder, but I'm not
sure what else. Nor is Bedford, her GP. We must
wait and see.'

Pip nodded. That meant tests and more tests,
and even then it wasn't always possible to be cer-
tain of the diagnosis and prognosis. She hoped it
was nothing serious because she liked Mrs Watts,
who never grumbled and who had made light of
her symptoms on the two occasions she had con-
sulted the surgeon.

Pip made herself useful as soon as she arrived
on Hamilton Ward, while her husband disappeared
into Sister's office. Wistfully, Pip watched his tall
figure, heard Sister's greeting, Hallam's laugh, then
the office door closed on them, and Pip was no
longer the consultant's wife, simply a volunteer
auxiliary.

A quick visit to all the surgical patients on that
block soon cheered her, and she saved Mrs Watts
for last.

She popped her head around the door as there was no reply to her knock, to find the patient crying quietly.

'Oh, it's you, Nurse,' Mrs Watts cried, holding out her arms.

Pip hugged her and gently smoothed back the thinning grey hair. 'It's all right. You will be well looked after here. There's every luxury, you know—even a colour TV if you want one!' Pip teased, and Mrs Watts cheered up a little.

'I wondered about the telly, but I couldn't see one.'

'They'll let you have one, if you ask. Some people aren't keen,' Pip explained.

Mrs Watts plucked nervously at her plain, thick nightie. 'I'm not used to such luxury,' she confided. 'I haven't any nice nighties, but I bought some slippers in Marks.'

Pip duly admired the pretty blue slippers. Certainly the nightgown was old and its colour now indeterminate. 'Can't your daughter buy you a new one?' she asked, remembering that Mrs Watts had a married daughter.

The woman shook her head. 'She's got three children to feed and clothe. Mick doesn't earn a lot. If I hadn't been saving up in a private insurance scheme, I wouldn't be here in the lap of luxury you know, Nurse!'

Pip smiled. Probably Mrs Watts would have been happier in the local hospital. She herself found such luxurious surroundings intimidating, but one became accustomed to money, she had found. Indeed, Pip wondered how she had ever managed without the allowance her husband made her. Of course, a lot of that went to Melanie, just as her salary had in the past.

'What will they do to me, Nurse?' Mrs Watts plucked pathetically at Pip's sleeve.

'Did Mr Fielding tell you what he'd decided?'

'Well ... he said he thought it was a touch of gall-bladder trouble. Some funny name he called it. Curly something.'

'Cholecystitis,' Pip put in, and Mrs Watts nodded.

'That was the word. I had that awful barium X-ray. My word! Shouldn't want that again!' To Pip's relief, Mrs Watts began to chuckle. After a few moments idle chat, Pip sought out Staff Nurse Le Maistre, and was soon hard at work helping bath the patients.

Only two needed a bed-bath, the rest went to one of the many spacious, well-appointed bath-rooms, where they did not always require nursing help. The doors did not lock, though, just in case, and a bell was strategically placed by the bath so patients could ring for assistance.

Although she couldn't do a lot to help the patients, the little nursing she *did* do whetted Pip's appetite. She simply must get back to complete her general training. She couldn't wait a whole year!

Of course, Hallam still had Sister Farrell, who was a mine of information regarding patients, treatments and operations, but Sister was glad of Pip's help because Hallam seemed to be taking on more patients than ever. He was working himself into an early grave, according to Sister Farrell, and Pip couldn't help noticing the sharp glance the Scotswoman had directed at her. As though the fault was Pip's.

And perhaps it was, she acknowledged, as she

collected the used bath-towels and piled them into the linen-skip. Since that dreadful evening when Pip had intended to make her husband want her, they had drifted further apart. She *did* try, on several occasions, to bridge the gap. It took two to make a marriage as well as to break it, but Hallam refused to meet her halfway, seeming always to be pulling in the opposite direction. If she commented on a patient's illness or treatment, all was well. They had many interesting, if stilted and formal, conversations about work. It was when Pip branched out into personal matters that Hallam shut up like a clam. She didn't dare mention his brother Geoff's name now. Once had been enough. The filthy look he gave her when she tentatively asked if the letter he was reading was from Geoffrey would have been enough to deter the most thick-skinned of wives. To sensitive Pip, the look spoke volumes. Leave Geoffrey alone and do not mention his name to me again. Hallam's sharp glance said that and much more.

So they rarely communicated now, and Pip became lonelier and lonelier. True, Alison was friendly, but she had her own studying to do. Sister Farrell was nearly of retiring age, and really Pip had little in common with her, so she made her own amusements. She took up knitting again, and had half finished a pullover for Simon. She decided six Ordinary levels wasn't sufficient and enrolled for Human Biology GCE with a correspondence school. And, most important, she spent a lot of time writing letters to schools of nursing for their brochures. Hallam said one year, but surely he wouldn't mind if it were less?

Some schools required Advanced levels, some

more than the certificates she possessed, but she had earmarked two that seemed suitable. She could not, naturally, live in and that was the problem. The hospital had to be within reasonable travelling distance of home. Public transport was good if Pip walked to the main road, but that was over a mile away and she would not fancy the walk in the cold, dark days of winter, particuarly when she was on nights.

The answer, of course, was a car. That she could not drive was a minor deterrent. She would take lessons. Hallam could not possibly object, as long as she didn't use *his* car.

But Hallam did object. His face darkened with anger, and Pip involuntarily took a step backwards. 'Can't I have lessons, then?' Realising why he wasn't enthusiastic, she hurried on: 'It wouldn't cost you anything. I could pay for lessons out of my allowance! Then I could save for a car. Just a secondhand one,' she murmured unhappily, as Hallam had still not spoken.

He shook his head, that troublesome lock falling over his left eye again. 'I'm not keen on the idea, Pip. Traffic is very heavy going up to London. Then there is the winter. No, I'm sorry.'

Pip turned sadly away. He was right about the traffic, she reflected, but she would have coped. The trouble with Hallam was that he didn't realise how self-sufficient his wife was.

Somehow the time dragged on. Pip continued her weekly visits to Hallam's clinic, on one occasion taking with her a pretty flowered brushed nylon nightie for Mrs Watts. She had hesitantly offered it to the patient, unwilling to cause her embarrass-

ment, and was overwhelmed by the woman's grati-
tude. It left a warm glow in Pip's heart, and made
her all the more determined to start her training as
soon as possible.

Mrs Watts duly had a successful operation and
was discharged but insisted that Pip visit her at
home whenever she could. Another obese lady was
admitted for a similar operation, and though she
was very different from Mrs Watts, Pip took the
old lady to her heart.

Mrs Fennell was over sixty, had several children
and seemingly hundreds of grandchildren, plus one
baby grandson. She was a moneyed woman, by all
accounts, but she wasn't snobbish as Pip had found
some of them were. She had a proud manner, but
a quiet dignity that endeared her to Pip. And she,
too, never complained, though she had bouts of
considerable pain and discomfort as the cholecystitis came and went. She was in a quiet stage at
the moment, which was better for surgery, and
Hallam had arranged to remove her gall-bladder.

Operating-theatre technique fascinated Pip, who
had not, as yet, been in a theatre. She knew she
would never want to become a theatre nurse because one never saw a conscious patient, and she
wouldn't feel involved. Yet the idea that she might
watch her dear Hallam operating grew on her.

When, tentatively, she made her request to Sister
Cartwright, the woman frowned. 'Usually Mr
Fielding doesn't like onlookers in the theatre, you
know. He says it isn't a free peep-show and that
unnecessary people pose extra problems.'

Pip's face fell, and Sister chuckled. 'I'm sure he
couldn't object to *you* watching! I'll see what I can
arrange with him.'

Pip would have preferred that Hallam wasn't asked. Surely she could just merge into the background? Being masked and gowned, he wouldn't know who she was anyway.

She was prepared for a curt refusal, and was overjoyed on her next visit to be told that she could watch, after all.

'He didn't mind?' she asked in surprise, and Sister put a finger to her lips.

'Well . . . I didn't ask, to tell you the truth! But the theatres have an overhead gallery, you know, where medical students and distinguished visitors can watch, without getting in the way,' Sister explained.

'I didn't know that, Sister. Could I watch from there?'

Sister nodded. 'It so happens that a group of young American doctors will be visiting the clinic on Thursday—the day of Mrs Fennell's cholecystectomy. You could merge with them, I should think. That way, we run no risk of antagonising Mr Fielding! As you must be aware, he has a *very* uncertain temper!' Sister smiled.

Oh, yes. I do know, Pip thought, but wisely kept silent. Hallam deserved her loyalty, if nothing else.

So it was arranged, and a nervous yet excited Pip made her lonely way up to the gallery on Thursday. If she hoped to slip in unnoticed, she was disappointed. The Americans were already there, as she knew they would be, and every head turned as the tiny, slender redhead made her way to her seat unobtrusively.

At least, Pip *tried* to be unobtrusive, but with so many admiring remarks and offers of help, that was out of the question!

She wore the plain white overall that she used on Mondays, but no cap, and her abundant wavy hair she left loose. It simply did not occur to her that the young doctors would admire her hair, or be taken by her sweet-natured face. She smiled politely at them, then gazed, entranced, at the scene below. The drama was about to begin. Why, it was like being in a *real* theatre!

The star, as far as she was concerned, was Hallam, but she knew that the most important person in the theatre was the patient. It was for the patient's benefit that the doctors and nurses and technicians were gathered below—a salutory lesson in humility for those too-proud sisters or consultants who saw themselves as king-pin.

They could see down into the theatre quite clearly, being separated from it only by glass. An intercom connected them with the floor below. The surgeon would, according to Sister, make helpful comments during the course of the operation, as he had an interested audience. Teaching was part of a senior surgeon's duties. Although Hallam did not like extraneous people in the theatre itself, he was always helpful to visiting colleagues provided they remained in the gallery.

Pip lost count of time. The only two people in the world were herself and Hallam. Even the patient on the operating table became unreal. She had eyes only for the surgeon. Despite his being gowned and masked, she picked him out easily. He was the tallest of the men there. The man opposite was, she presumed, his assistant. Next to Hallam the tall, angular figure of Sister Theatre was visible. At the patient's head, the anaesthetist was busy. It was probably Dr Stewart, whom she had met briefly.

Pip spared a thought for Mrs Fennell, for whose benefit this was all laid on. Not that Mrs Fennell was visible. She was just a body on the table, her head in the capable care of Dr Stewart, the rest of her body covered, allowing exposure only of the operation site.

Suddenly the intercom crackled and she heard Hallam's voice. He was, he explained, about to perform a routine cholecystectomy, which Pip knew was removal of the gall-bladder. The patient was in her late sixties, obese, but otherwise in good health. He expected no difficulties but reminded his audience that one must always expect the unexpected and be prepared.

He went on, very briefly, to describe his technique for the particular operation, then there was silence as the op began, and Pip let her breath out in a great sigh.

She found her hands were clenched, her palms sweating. The tension was unbearable—yet to Hallam it was just so much routine. If only he could feel her love winging its way down to him! If only he knew how she cared. He thought her to be a sex-craxy young girl, wanting him yet laughing at him at the same time because of his age.

Oh, Hallam! she cried to herself. I *do* love you, and you will never know.

The op seemed to go on for hours but Pip hardly moved, unlike the doctors, who, although as interested as herself, occasionally shuffled their feet or gave a discreet cough. Once or twice she heard a slight crunching. Presumably someone had brought his own popcorn!

Eventually, Hallam held out his hand for the needle and thread, and his audience sat back, nodding and whispering to one another. Pip almost burst with pride. It was *her* Hallam they were praising!

Then there was hurried movement in the theatre below, and all eyes in the gallery swivelled downward, as something seemed to be going wrong.

Pip held her breath, not daring to take her eyes off Hallam. The anaesthetist was juggling about with his machine, nurses were coming forward . . . Pip could bear no more. Poor Mrs Fennell must have died and her Hallam would be blamed! White-faced and feeling very, very sick, Pip shut her eyes tightly and hung her head. She could not look, she simply could not. Instead, she superstitiously crossed her fingers and begged it to be all right. Perhaps the machine had faulted, perhaps . . .

She could hear nothing from the American doctors, and she risked a glance at them. All were watching the scene below with rapt attention. They, too, were holding their breath and waiting, hoping. So Pip closed her eyes again. It must be her fault that there was a crisis down there. She should never have come. Hallam was right in not wanting non-essential people in the theatre and if he knew she was here he would tell her that the gallery was out of bounds, too.

Time passed and still the Americans watched, still Pip sat with downcast eyes. She began to pray. Although not a religious girl, she felt someone must hear her.

Movement started again in the gallery, and Pip flicked her eyes open—to find a young, freckle-faced doctor leaning towards her solicitously. 'You O.K.?' he whispered, and Pip nodded, then pointed to the theatre. She mouthed the words 'Is it all right now?' and he gave her the thumbs-up sign.

Pip gave her informant a tremulous smile, and he leaned nearer. Hesitantly, she glanced through the glass partition, not sure what she would see. She was in time to see the patient being wheeled out of the theatre with nurses and the anaesthetist in attendance. Mrs Fennell was alive then.

Hallam's weary voice came through the inter-com, explaining the surgical crisis in terms only doctors could understand, but Pip let it wash over her. Mrs Fennell was alive and her dear Hallam had saved her! That it must have been a team effort she did not consider. As long as Hallam was there, the patient would survive.

She leaned further forward, just as Hallam glanced up—their eyes met, and Pip hurriedly shot back again. Surely he wouldn't recognise her from this distance? But her red hair was unmistakable. He couldn't possibly have missed her, and the freckle-faced doctor chose that moment to slip a comforting arm around her shoulders.

'Are you sure you're O.K.? You seem awfully pale. The patient a friend of yours?' His arm was still about her as she hurriedly rose and followed the others out. She risked another glance down, but Hallam was sitting on a stool in the theatre. He did not look up again.

Although she didn't want to seem rude, Pip was anxious to get away from the young doctor, whose name, he told her, was Bill Smith. 'There's a good old American name for you!' he drawled, and Pip tried to join in his laughter but all the excitement, then the tension and fear had been too much, and she burst into tears.

She found her head resting on the doctor's broad

shoulder, and her tears being gently wiped away as they fell. And there were a great many of them. The dam had burst at last and all Pip's pent-up emotions were let loose like flood-water.

She began hesitantly to apologise, but Bill shrugged good-naturedly. 'You must have needed that cry,' he murmured against her hair, and she nodded.

'It was all too much,' she whispered, then pulled away from him, aware of an interested audience. The visitors were being herded together by a small, bustling man Pip did not know, and Bill reluctantly left her, after giving her arm a final squeeze. She assured him that she worked in the clinic and that her ward Sister would look after her.

She turned, uncertain whether to return to Hamilton ward or get a taxi straight home, when Bill came back. 'I've fixed it with the little guy. Said I would take you back to your ward and catch up with them later.'

Pip, horrified, opened her mouth to protest, but Bill just smiled kindly, and, taking her arm, gently propelled her towards the surgical unit. 'Which ward was it?'

'H . . .' she began, then turned on a bright smile to reassure him. 'I really am perfectly all right, Dr Smith. I'll just put my overall in the laundry-room then go home. I was due off, anyway,' she assured him, but his jaw jutted forward pugnaciously, and Pip's smile faltered. Evidently Dr Smith considered it his duty to take her back to her ward, and he intended doing his duty, come what may.

A defeated Pip allowed him to shepherd her to Hamilton ward. Dr Smith placed her in the care of Sister Cartwright who gave him a sharp glance when she saw the tender look he bestowed on Pip. Swallowing her surprise and disapproval, Sister promised to see that Pip had a rest before going home. Finally, after what seemed hours, Bill Smith rejoined his colleagues, and Pip, crushed and unable to take any more, subsided into a chair.

'I'm sorry, Sister, but I became unwell in the gallery and ... and Dr Smith was so kind! But I couldn't get rid of him,' she finished miserably. Sister was bound to tell Hallam about the young American and Pip felt she must get the picture straight now, or heaven only knew what Hallam would think!

'What sort of unwell?' Sister asked gently, automatically reaching for Pip's wrist. Surprised, Pip allowed her pulse to be taken. She guessed it must be back to normal by now.

'Oh, sort of faint and ... and sick, I suppose,' she said. 'It was all the drama, Sister. What happened? Was Mrs Fennell all right?' she asked anxiously. For a few moments she had forgotten all about the crisis. 'And poor Hallam. He was sitting on a stool. I saw him! He must be so weary!' she cried, trying to get up, but Sister Cartwright was a big woman, and Pip found herself sitting down again with Sister's arms restraining her.

'You mustn't get worked up, Mrs Fielding. The patient is rather poorly, but she should pull through. She's a tough old lady,' Sister added. 'And Mr Fielding was understandably tired after all that. Surgeons have to be tough, you know, with strong legs and a good back. But even for the toughest of them, it's hard work. Naturally he sat down once he had the opportunity. Wouldn't you?'

Pip nodded, relieved. He was understandably weary. That was the obvious explanation. Still, she would be happier once she had seen him. She got up as a nurse came into the office, glad of the opportunity to escape. She was aware of Sister calling after her, but pretended to be deaf. The sooner she got out of there the better!

Exhausted, Pip paid off the taxi and let herself into the house. She could hear a faint rattle of crockery from the kitchen, but apart from that the house was quiet. She must lie down, have a cat-nap.

But it was late afternoon when Pip awoke from her dream-filled sleep—to find Hallam sitting silently by her bed. She half sat up, instantly worried. Why was he here? Had something happened?

'Are you ill?' she breathed, as he remained silent.

There was a peculiar expression on his lean face, and an odd smile turned up the corners of his mouth. 'No, I'm just tired. I had a busy morning, Pip. And you? Sister Cartwright thought you unwell.'

Pip shook her head vigorously. 'Oh, no! I'm fine, really. It was just the shock. I came over faint, but I'm all right now. Truly,' she hastened to reassure him, her deep blue eyes fixed on his tired face.

'Sister told me you had nausea,' he stated flatly, and Pip frowned. There was something amiss here. Hallam wasn't angry, yet . . .

It was difficult to judge his moods, he was such a changeable man. 'I did feel a bit sick,' Pip acknowledged, 'but only because I thought you'd killed Mrs Fennell,' she went on candidly, then heard a sharp explosion of sound. Her eyes widened in disbelief, as Hallam fought for control. She felt sure he was going to hit her, and she flinched away.

'You thought I had *what*?' he asked, biting each word out between clenched teeth.

'I meant that . . . that I thought Mrs Fennell had died. And . . . and I thought . . .' Pip's voice wavered, then died away. She still wasn't positive that Hallam wouldn't beat her.

He began to pace the floor like a caged wild animal, and all sorts of thoughts flashed through Pip's brain. He was so angry he was going to divorce her! That was it, he wished now he had wed Vanessa. Pip didn't suppose that Vanessa would be foolish enough to accuse Hallam of killing a patient.

'You thought Mrs Fennell had died on the table and that I was responsible for her death? Was that the message your muddled brain was trying to send to your tongue?' Hallam enquired acidly, and Pip nodded. He didn't need to be so unkind about it.

'The op went splendidly. There was a crisis at the end but all was resolved satisfactorily,' he said.

'But . . . but I thought she died! I mean,' Pip blundered on, 'you were all rushing towards her and I thought she had died and you would be blamed,' she finished in a small voice then turned away from him and sank back against the pillows, closing her eyes firmly. Hopefully, he would take the hint.

But he did not. Because her eyes were closed, she was unaware of the tenderness in his own as he tentatively rubbed his forefinger across the bridge of her small, straight nose.

'Oh!' Startled, she sat bolt upright, and Hallam raised a bushy brow, his glance amused.

'I didn't mean to frighten you, Pip. Did it matter to you that I might be blamed?' His gaze held hers, and she smiled shyly. Surely now he must realise how deep her feelings were? She nodded, unable to find words.

'Sister was rather worried about you. She kept on about the nausea and pointed out it was during the morning,' Hallam went on reflectively, and a small frown marred the smoothness of Pip's forehead.

'Don't frown, Pip. You will get lines, like me.' Gently, Hallam smoothed away the frown, his fingers cool and refreshing on Pip's flushed face.

'What has morning got to do with my nausea?' Pip asked, innocently, and a sardonic smile crossed her husband's face.

'Morning sickness, Pip. Sister smiled coyly at me and said she wondered if I had any news for her,' Hallam finished drily, his eyes never leaving Pip's face.

'Oh!' Full realisation hit Pip. How could she have been so stupid! Sister believed her to be pregnant! Swift tides of colour suffused her pale skin, as Hallam watched, apparently fascinated. The longer he watched, the more she blushed, and she hit out at him with the only weapon she had—her tongue.

'She need not have worried then, need she? Pregnant is the last thing I would be!' Pip cried.

Hallam's face closed up, and she was immediately ashamed. Now she had hurt him. Of course, she argued with herself, she had intended to hurt him, so why be upset about it?

'I could hardly tell Sister Cartwright that,' he pointed out reasonably, and Pip had to agree.

'Were you cross? I mean, about her hinting at such a thing?'

'Embarrassed rather than cross,' he said, his voice chilly. 'A man of my age getting a young girl pregnant is not something to be proud of.'

'But we're married!' Pip wailed, unhappy because now *he* was hurting her with words.

'So we are, so we are,' he murmured, then glanced at his watch. 'As long as you are well, Pip. I just wanted to be sure. Don't wait dinner,' he added, already halfway out of the bedroom door, 'I have a dinner engagement.' Then the door closed, and Pip was alone.

She pressed her hands to her still-burning cheeks. A baby, Hallam's baby! No, it wasn't possible. She definitely wasn't pregnant. If she was then Hallam would have to pay her more attention, wouldn't he? *Then* he wouldn't go off to some dinner engagement. Was he taking Vanessa out to some swell restaurant, then on to a club for dancing, a few drinks, a long, lingering goodnight?

Her lips tightened. That's exactly what he was doing! She had thought, before their marriage, that once they were wed Hallam wouldn't bother to take her out anywhere, and she was perfectly right. She hadn't been out in the evening since. Yet he squired Vanessa around at least twice a week, she felt sure of that.

Hallam's baby. The more she dwelt on the idea, the better it seemed. A baby on whom she could pour all the love she longed to give Hallam. He neither needed her love nor her, but a baby would appreciate it. Would, indeed, demand love and care as a right. Pip clasped her hands across her stomach, as if she could already feel new life there.

The problem was Hallam himself. Once before she had thrown herself at him. She smiled at memory of their wedding night. Then her young face darkened. Finding her new husband breakfasting with his mistress the morning after wasn't something she cared to remember! If Hallam intended to pass on his seed, he would want Vanessa to bear the children. That was perfectly obvious. For Pip he had nothing but contempt.

Pip's agile mind worked on a solution to the problem for almost a week, but quickly discarded scheme after scheme. Hallam patently didn't want her, so there was simply no point in bothering. Then an unexpected guest turned up.

Pip was arranging flowers and autumn leaves in the hall when there was a hearty thumping at the front door. Not wanting to bother the housekeeper, Pip opened it—to find Geoffrey Fielding on the doorstep, case in hand.

' 'Tis young Pip!' he shouted, gathering her into his arms for a brotherly hug.

'Oh, Geoff!' Pip cried, feeling the tears pricking her eyelids. No, she mustn't cry. It was selfish, and unfair to Geoffrey.

'Hallam never said you were coming.' A delighted Pip ushered her brother-in-law in, then she tapped at the study door. Hallam would be writing his lecture-notes. Without waiting for a reply, she popped her head around the door. 'Look who's here!'

Geoffrey's head and broad shoulders followed her, and both of them beamed at Hallam, who rose quickly. In his agitation, he knocked over a small table piled with books, then swore.

Pip and Geoffrey exchanged worried glances, and Hallam chose that moment to look up, a smile fixed to his face. Then it died as he believed he saw two young people, in love with each other. A hopeless love because he was in their way.

CHAPTER NINE

PIP left the brothers to a good old gossip while she made the coffee. The coldness in her heart had been replaced by a warm glow. Geoffrey would understand her plight, he would offer a helping hand. He, above all, would help her to understand his brother's changeable nature. Hallam blew hot and cold. One never knew quite what he was going to do next.

She hummed a little tune as she set out cups and saucers. There ought to be a few biscuits somewhere. Ah, yes, shortbread. Geoffrey would like that. Still placidly humming to herself, she was about to tap on the study door, which was ajar, when Hallam's cold voice stopped her in her tracks.

'It's been a ghastly mistake, Geoffrey. A nightmare! A long, dark tunnel with no light at the end,' he went on, more quietly. So quietly that Pip had to strain to catch the words.

Unashamed of eavesdropping, she stood like a statue, waiting for the next words. It concerned her, of that she was sure. If she knew, *really* knew how Hallam felt it might help her to understand him.

'It wasn't such a mistake, old man,' Geoffrey's hearty voice broke in, and she heard Hallam grunt.

'I wish,' her husband continued, 'that I had never set eyes on the girl.'

Pip's mouth made a big 'O' of despair, but she

closed it before a sound could emerge. Listeners never hear well of themselves, she chided herself, as she silently pushed the trolley back as far as the kitchen door. Then, whistling tunelessly, she went forward again and pushed the study door with her foot. Geoffrey rose immediately and took the trolley from her, warming her with his smile as he did so. Hallam was staring down at the fireplace and gave no sign that he knew she was in the room.

'The cup that cheers, Pip. You make me feel I'm a welcome guest!' Geoffrey smiled, and Pip returned the smile, but with her lips only.

'H . . . Hallam didn't say you were coming. Are you staying long? We haven't got a room ready. Or . . . or anything,' she went on wildly. Oh, please, Hallam! *Say* something, she begged silently, but he went on staring at the fire, far away from them both.

Pip and Geoffrey exchanged glances, then, head bent, Pip trundled the trolley out, closing the door firmly behind her.

Geoffrey still hadn't said how long he would be stopping but Pip hoped it would be a long visit. Getting a room ready for him would give her something to do, keep her hands occupied, but not her mind. That still dwelt on the problem of how to make Hallam appreciate her. If she couldn't have his baby, she must find some other way . . . An illness, that would do! She must become ill, then Hallam wouldn't take Vanessa out for a week or two, perhaps not ever again.

It was tempting fate to pretend to be ill when you were perfectly fit, but she was desperate. She would do anything, *anything* at all to win more time with her husband. She couldn't win his love, for hadn't she heard him with her own ears? *It's a ghastly mistake. I wish I had never set eyes on the girl!* Pip, too, wished she had never set eyes on the lean, dark man she had come to love. Far better that their paths had never crossed.

Pip was sitting quietly on the verandah when Geoffrey found her. She felt a large, square hand descend on her shoulder, and she gave him a wan smile.

'Thought I would find you here, young Pip,' he said, heartily, too heartily, and she gave him a reproachful look.

'Sorry. Didn't mean to sound like an out-of-season Father Christmas!'

'Well, you did,' she cried, blue eyes full of anguish and unshed tears. Then she was in his arms, being comforted, in a way Hallam never thought to do.

Gently, her brother-in-law stroked her hair. 'It's a beautiful colour, Pip. Not many men have a wife with hair like that. Hallam ought to be proud.'

She pulled away and managed a wan smile. Best to keep up the pretence. It wasn't fair to Geoffrey to lumber him with her marital problems. And, she told herself firmly, it wasn't fair to his unpredictable brother.

Unconsciously, she held her head a little higher, and tilted her chin defiantly. 'Hallam *is* proud of my hair,' she lied, avoiding Geoffrey's concerned gaze.

But he wouldn't let her go as easily as that. He caught hold of her cold hand and warmed it between his own. 'There isn't much I can do for you, Pip,' he began. 'Hallam is . . .'

Pip snatched her hand away as Hallam appeared

from the sitting-room. 'I shall be out most of the afternoon. There's a consultants' meeting at the hospital,' he said, his keen gaze going from Pip to Geoffrey, and back.

Pip felt herself redden, then anger overcame her embarrassment. Why should *she* feel guilty? She hadn't anything to reproach herself for. It was Hallam who spent his spare time in the arms of another woman. 'You'll stay for lunch?' she asked, struggling to hold down her resentment, but Hallam shook his head.

'No, I'll grab a bite in the canteen.' He seemed about to say more, then closed his mouth firmly and strode away.

Pip bit her lip. He was lunching with Vanessa! She was sure of it.

'Does he often disappear for the day, Pip?' Geoffrey asked gently, and she shook her head.

'Only occasionally. He's a busy man,' she defended, and Geoffrey chuckled.

'Tell you what, when I've got some of the travel-dust washed off, we'll go out to lunch. Or dinner, if you prefer?'

'No. Hallam wouldn't like it.'

'Does that matter?' Geoffrey probed.

'Of course it does,' she cried. 'He . . . he might be hurt,' she finished. Or would he care either way?

'You love him then?'

She forced herself to meet Geoffrey's serious blue-grey eyes, then nodded, too full to speak.

'That's a good sign, Pip. Once he comes to terms with himself, he will be grateful for that. Never stop loving him.'

Surprised, she began to ask why, then thought

better of it. Geoffrey knew Hallam far better than she did. If he decided that Hallam would be glad of her love one day she wouldn't question it.

'I wonder if brother Hallam really has got a consultants' meeting?' he went on, and she turned on him, angry because she'd been wondering the very same thing, and they were both being disloyal to Hallam.

'He wouldn't go off and leave you!' she snapped. 'Of course he has a meeting.' Annoyed, she began to tear bits off the magazine she'd been pretending to read. When she glanced up again, she was alone. Naturally there must be a consultants' meeting. They met regularly. Hallam might have made some excuse if there had been just Pip and himself for lunch but he wouldn't leave his brother just like that. Would he?

No. She pushed away the disloyal thought. He would be back directly after the meeting, in plenty of time for dinner.

Pip elected to prepare dinner that evening— Chicken Maryland. She knew Hallam enjoyed chicken, and only hoped her cooking ability was up to his standard. The chicken was almost ready when the telephone shrilled. She tensed, then berated herself for a fool. It had rung several times during the day. It wasn't necessarily Hallam ringing to say he wouldn't be in for dinner.

Geoffrey answered it, spoke briefly, then peered around the kitchen door. 'Brother Hallam. Might be late. Do not wait dinner,' he repeated verbatim, and Pip flinched.

She stared down at the fruit. 'His Chicken Maryland will be spoiled,' she whispered, eyes downcast. 'He could have postponed whatever he had to do,' she went on, turning to Geoffrey. 'Couldn't he?'

Geoffrey shrugged. 'A doctor's life is an unpredictable one, Pip. He didn't say where he was, but from the sounds in the background I should say he was at the clinic.'

Pip brightened. 'Then he'll get a meal when he's finished, won't he? I'll save him some chicken, just in case.' If Hallam was at the clinic, he couldn't be in Vanessa's arms.

They were playing chess when Hallam eventually returned, his face lined and haggard. Impulsively, Pip jumped up, meaning to run to him, smooth away the lines of fatigue, the strain, then quickly she drew her hand back. Hallam wouldn't want her to touch him. 'I'll get you some coffee,' she said instead, but he put a restraining hand on her arm. The contact was more than she could bear and she tried surreptitiously to extricate herself. Geoffrey was gazing fixedly at the chess-men, apparently taking no notice of the little scene, and she silently sent him her thanks.

Hallam's hand tightened. 'I could do with a large Scotch,' he said harshly, and she nodded. His hand fell away and he disappeared in the direction of his study.

Pip poured him a large whisky, then added a little soda. Although not a great drinker, Hallam clearly needed something strong now. He looked ghastly.

'Want me to take it in, Pip?'

'No-o. I will. Though I don't doubt he would prefer your company to mine,' she replied, with unconscious bitterness.

Geoffrey heaved a sigh. 'Think I'll turn in then.

It's been a long day. Must keep my brain fresh for the conference tomorrow. Night, Pip.' He planted a kiss on the top of her head and she swallowed. He was so *kind*, so considerate, so ... So everything Hallam was not, but she had married Hallam knowing full well that he did not love her, did not even like her. She was simply 'more readily available' as he put it. She couldn't complain. Her love must be enough for them both.

Crying inwardly, Pip tapped at the study door, then crept in, deposited the whisky glass on a small table within reach of Hallam's hand, and was about to creep out when his voice stopped her.

'Geoffrey still about?' As well as looking strained and tired, he sounded it too, and Pip's heart flipped. He needed comforting, yet she would be rebuffed if she offered that comfort. Only Vanessa could soothe him.

At that moment if it had been within Pip's power to produce Vanessa, she would have done so. If Vanessa could bring a smile to his haggard face, then let him have her! 'I ... he's gone to bed, Hallam,' she whispered, hesitantly moving nearer. 'He said he wanted to keep his brain fresh for the conference. He ... shall I ask him to come down?'

Hallam grunted, and she hovered, not sure if that particular grunt meant Yes or No. Then his tired, dark gaze flicked over her. It held no animosity, only a deep, deep sorrow, and Pip could bear it no longer. Forgetting that he hated her and would angrily fling her away, she hurried over to his armchair, knelt by his side and took one of his lean, strong hands in between her own. 'Won't I do? To lend you a shoulder to cry on, I mean? I ... I am your wife,' Pip hurried on, not wanting to give him the chance of rejecting her.

Hallam picked up the glass and drained it in one gulp while Pip knelt there, still imprisoning his other hand. Her eyes widened as he stared at the glass, commenting that he could do with another one.

'Oh, no! No, you mustn't!' Aghast, she sprang up and put the glass out of his reach. 'Drinking won't solve your problems! Please, won't you let me help you?' She resumed her position by his knees, gazing up trustingly. 'I promise not to be silly or ... or anything,' she went on, quickly, hiding her flushed face. I mean that I won't throw myself at you, she said silently, but could not bring herself to frame the words.

'Do I need a shoulder to cry on?' he asked, his free hand idly stroking the silky red hair.

Heat shot through her at his touch. If he could do that by just touching her hair, what might he do to her emotions if he touched her body? And she wanted him to touch her, wanted to feel his strong yet gentle hands caressing her, loving her ... But it would be only a basic animal hunger for him. Not love. Never love.

'I thought you looked awful when you came in,' she said frankly, and was rewarded by a faint laugh.

'You do great things for my ego, Pip!' he commented, then went on soberly: 'I lost a patient.'

'No!' She twisted round so that she could see his dear face. Dark grey eyes met blue ones, as she gazed earnestly up at him. Gently, he traced the outline of her mouth with one finger. 'You remember David Ives?'

She nodded, too tense to speak.

'He died this afternoon. That's where I was.'

'The . . . ulcer. Did it perforate?'

'Mm. Such a vital man. In the prime of life,' he mused, half to himself.

Pip squirmed, wishing Hallam would take his hand away from her face, where his thumb was now gently probing a pulse spot.

Abruptly he removed his hand, just as she had wished, and stared at the wall.

Pip hesitantly laid her head on his thigh, and settled herself more comfortably. She dared not close her eyes, for any moment he would remember that she was Pip, not Vanessa, and that he couldn't stand the sight of her.

A tremor shot through her as those long, surgeon's fingers entangled themselves in her hair, then inched their way down gently to the back of her neck, where they stayed half-encircling her throat. She tensed, waiting for him to fling her away, to bruise and maim her with his words, but he did not.

Some of the tension left her, and she gave a small, kittenish sigh.

'You sounded almost happy, Pip,' Hallam said gently, his hand moving up to her hair again.

'I'm warm and comfortable!' she retorted, unwilling to tell him how he could make her even happier. Best not to appear too content. He didn't seem to want, or expect her to be happy.

'I'm sorry about Mr Ives,' she went on, her voice muffled as she pressed her face closer to his leg. Don't send me away yet,' she begged silently. I'm content here. And comfortable. And I feel at home.

'I'm sorry, too. It is always a blow to lose a

patient. But we must keep a sense of proportion, Pip. Most patients survive major surgery. Only a few fall by the wayside.'

'I know. But I'm still sorry,' she whispered. 'He was getting on a bit, though, wasn't he?' So perhaps death wasn't the blow it would be to someone of her own age.

Hallam's hand stilled, and she felt his mental withdrawal. Obviously she had said the wrong thing. She looked up, but he was staring at the wallpaper again, a muscle working at the corner of his wide mouth. 'He was a year younger than me, Pip,' he said coldly, and she began to stammer an apology.

Abruptly he shook himself free and stood up, pulling her with him. 'I'm tired. It's time I got my beauty sleep. After all, old men like me shouldn't stay up too late!' He gave a harsh laugh, and Pip stepped back as if he'd struck her.

'I'm sorry, Hallam. I didn't mean that . . . that you . . . I mean, he *looked* old!' she stammered out, trying desperately to soothe him. 'I didn't mean . . . that is, I . . . you're not old!' she got out at last, and a faint, self-derisive smile touched his mouth.

'No, not old, merely middle-aged. Far too old for a girl of twenty,' he said bitterly.

'No! No, you're not middle-aged!' Aghast, she sprang at him, pressing her body close to his coldly unresponsive one. 'Please, Hallam. Don't send me away,' she whispered clinging even harder to him. Greatly daring, she moved her hands along what she could reach of his spine, and snuggled her head against his shirt. Through the thin material she could hear his heart beating rhythmically. He didn't care! He was untouched by her nearness, by her plea. He might as well be a block of granite!

'Pip, don't,' he whispered, bending his head down so she could hear his words. She leaned back so that she could gaze into his eyes, see his dear face.

If he had looked ghastly when he returned home, he looked even worse now, if that was possible. His dark eyes were filled with torment, the harsh planes of his face working as though with some inner anguish.

'Pip,' he murmured, then she felt his heart-beat quicken as his body became aroused with desire for her.

Fiercely his mouth came down on hers, and a tremor shot through them both. Eagerly she parted her lips and pushed herself closer to him. He did care, after all! He wanted her! It wasn't love, but she must not be greedy. Perhaps in time he would come to love her. Time was all she needed. She would *make* him love her.

His hands moved sensuously over her body, exciting her, arousing her. She was filled with love and a deep longing for her husband. Surely he wouldn't push her away this time? Might not the ecstasy of their wedding-night be repeated?

His arms tightened, then he lifted her up and sat down in the big arm-chair, pulling Pip on to his lap. There she snuggled up to his chest, not daring to look up. She gave a faint murmur of contentment as his thumb caressed the pulse behind her ear.

'You are beginning to grow on me, Pip,' he murmured into her hair.

'Like a fungus, do you mean?' she asked, laughter in her voice.

'Could be!' he teased, his voice deep with emotion.

'I'm glad. I want to grow on you. I want to stay here, like this, for ever and ever,' Pip insisted, tilting her head back so she could see his expression.

He looked better, the torment was gone from his eyes. In some strange way he appeared younger, too, as if a great weight had been lifted from his shoulders.

Impulsively she pressed her soft, warm mouth to his, half-kneeling on his lap, and he gathered her fiercely to him, his arms tightening so that Pip could hardly breathe.

Feverishly she abandoned herself to their mutual passion, winding her arms around his neck, moulding her body to his. But their clothes were a barrier, and Pip felt his hands unbuttoning her shirt-waist dress. Then she cried out in ecstasy as his sensitive fingers caressed her young, firm breasts through the thin bra.

Her dress was rapidly discarded, her undies, too, and she lay back in Hallam's arms, quivering with love as he delicately explored the soft contours of her body. One hand cupped her breast while the other went on a tantalising exploration of her hips, her flat stomach.

The pleasure was unbearable. This wasn't a repetition of their wedding-night, it was a thousand times better. She longed for complete fulfilment, hungered for Hallam's body, his love. No, not love, she thought again, a wistful smile playing about her rosebud mouth.

'Something amusing you, my darling,' Hallam said huskily, both hands returning to her breasts, and she gasped as his lips teased her nipples.

'I ... I was just wishing you loved me,' she managed before his mouth claimed hers again, and eagerly she abandoned herself to the demands of his body.

His lips branded hers again, marking her out as Hallam's woman, then he, too, began to remove his clothes. Feeling wanton and deliciously wicked she helped him, her movements hasty. He must make love to her before he had time to stop and think, to consider what he was doing. He must take her *now*, before he changed back into the cold, autocratic consultant!

Then he was free of restrictions, and time had no meaning as he caressed her anew, bringing her to such heights of pleasure that it became unbearable.

Then the telephone shrilled, and they froze, like two statues.

Hallam gave a kind of shuddering gasp, and said, wryly: 'Saved by the bell.' Gently, he put her from him, snatched up his trousers and shirt and hurried out to the hall.

Pip sat up and hugged her knees to her, the longing for fulfilment too much to bear. Her whole body ached for him yet he had calmly put her to one side. Saved by the bell. What did that mean?

Dry-eyed, she began to dress, the unassuaged hunger still burning inside her. It was obvious what it meant. Hallam had been trapped by his own need of a woman, any woman. The telephone had saved him from doing something he would have regretted for weeks afterwards—making love to his own wife.

'I shall operate next Wednesday.' Hallam's calm

voice soothed Angela Robertson, while Pip stood demurely by. This was her other self, the efficient clinic-nurse in white overall and cap, assisting the debonair consultant.

Two weeks had passed since that awful night, the night when Pip had almost been made love to. The night she had lain awake until the next day dawned, her body on fire, filled with longing for Hallam. Filled with despair, too. For she knew now that she could not go on. His moment of weakness was because he needed a woman, someone to soothe him after the traumatic loss of a patient he hadn't expected to die. It need not have been his wife, any woman would have done as well. Vanessa, perhaps. *She* would have known immediately how to deal with the situation. She and Hallam must have had many similar little episodes.

Her mind only half on her work, Pip smilingly showed Miss Robertson out. The past two weeks had been busy ones. To her surprise she had been invited for interview at a nurse training school some seventy miles or so away, and, defiantly, she had gone to the interview and apparently impressed the PNO, Education with her enthusiasm and quiet determination. The fact that her husband was a highly-regarded consultant must have impressed them, too.

Naturally, they wanted to know how she could manage the training and still be a wife to the consultant. Without so much as a blush she had lied and assured them her husband had no objection to her living in while she trained. A daily journey of that distance was out of the question, but she would go home on her off-duty. She would manage perfectly well, she'd said airily.

Yes, she *would* manage, because she would not be returning home on her days off. Students were required to live in during their basic Introductory Block, unless domestic commitments prevented their doing so, but after that were free to live out. Pip hoped to get a bed-sitter or small flat near the hospital so that no-one would know she never went home.

Home. An evocative word. It conjured up visions of a warm, cosy sitting-room, a log fire blazing in the hearth, a man's loving arms . . .

And now she must tell Hallam, for the PNO had written to tell her that once satisfactory references had been obtained, Pip could start. Although the hospital would not, of course, ask Hallam for a reference as an employer, they would drop him a line out of courtesy. She balled her fists, pressing them to her mouth. She was back in her office now, the electric typewriter on her desk silent and condemning. She knew she ought to start Hallam's reports. Then there were his lecture-notes. He would be away in the Midlands for three days at some conference, similar to the one Geoffrey had attended in London.

Geoffrey . . . He was so kind and understanding, but she could not involve him in her troubles. He had confided that he was going steady with a local farmer's daughter. 'She has a loving nature, Pip. Just like you,' he'd said solemnly, and Pip had burst into tears and fled to the safety of her lonely bedroom.

A loving nature and no-one to love! What good was that?

Busy with her thoughts, she didn't hear Hallam and jumped when his hands descended on her thin shoulders. She turned, a question in her eyes. Whatever he wanted it would be to do with business. They never discussed personal matters now. 'Miss Robertson, Pip. What did you think about her?'

She frowned. 'Was there anything special to think about her? I mean, she seemed straightforward enough. A bit pale, though.'

Hallam nodded, dropping his hands. 'She isn't anaemic though. Her lab. tests were all right. What are the signs of anaemia, Pip?'

Pip smiled. This was safe territory. Hallam was good at teaching, taking great pains to see that she knew what each of his patients was suffering from, their signs and symptoms, and probable prognosis. Perhaps this was the time to tell him about St Mary's Hospital?

'They are generally pale, but being pale doesn't necessarily indicate anaemia,' she said hesitantly. Should she tell him now? 'Ah . . . the lips and nail-pads and just inside the eye are all pale.' Go on, Pip. *Now*, before your courage deserts you. 'The nails may be . . .' She stopped, and Hallam shot her a puzzled glance.

'I . . . The nails may be spoon-shaped . . . Hallam, I'm going to do my general!' she blurted out, all thoughts of anaemia vanishing from her mind.

He raised a bushy brow, his face otherwise expressionless. 'I wondered when I was to be told,' he commented mildly.

'You . . . you know?'

He nodded. 'The Principal Tutor and I served our apprenticeship at the same hospital. She was a third-year student nurse, I a humble student doctor. We knew each other quite well,' he went on, smiling reminiscently, and Pip gasped.

'She . . . she got in touch with you? She didn't say she knew you,' she went on, forlornly, and Hallam sent her a sharp look.

'Does it matter that she knows me? I should have imagined quite the contrary. It will smooth the way for you.'

'I don't want the way smoothed for me!' Pip wailed. 'I have to make my own way. If I'm useless, I expect to be shown the door. If I'm praised, it should be because I'm praiseworthy, not because the PNO was an old girl-friend!'

'Girl-friend? Was she?' Hallam sounded suspiciously as though he was laughing at her. 'She was—and is—a good friend, shall we say?' he said blandly, and Pip was left to make what she could of *that* remark.

'I hope you aren't angry?' she said belatedly, but he shrugged.

'Does it matter if I am? Does it bother you that I shall be without a nurse when Sister Farrell finally retires? That I will have to find a new secretary, a new receptionist? Perhaps a new wife?' he finished, still in that irritating, reasoned tone as though talking to a child.

The remark about a new wife struck Pip like a heavy blow, and she mentally reeled. Vanessa Clifton was waiting in the wings, the understudy eager to take over once the star had gone. Yet Pip had never been Hallam's star. She was only a substitute, a useful woman to have as a wife, but no more than that. Vanessa was the real star. Pip hoped the other woman would make Hallam happier than she herself had.

Pip was about to say so when Alison, Hallam's niece, came skipping in. She was bubbling over, her intelligent eyes behind the tinted spectacles glowing with vitality and excitement.

'Uncle Hallam! Pip! Caught you in time. Andrew and I are just going into town, but I wanted to tell you, well, Pip, anyway—we're going to have a baby!'

'Alison! That's splendid news.' Hallam went forward and kissed his niece on her brow, while Pip struggled to hide her anguish.

A baby. If only *she* were having a baby! 'I'm so pleased,' she said shyly, and Alison came over and hugged her.

'Thought you intellectuals didn't believe in motherhood!' Hallam joked, his irritation gone.

'I didn't before I was married, I must say,' his niece admitted. 'But it's a wonderful feeling. To think there is actually someone growing in here,' she patted her abdomen. 'A real person!' She seemed unable to quite believe it herself, and chatted away to her uncle while Pip busied herself tidying the desk.

She would have to get the knitting-needles out. Pip enjoyed knitting. It would be poignant, making baby-clothes just as though *she* were pregnant, but she liked Alison and must do all she could for her. Primrose was a safe enough colour, she mused, their conversation washing over her. A primrose pants and jacket suit, perhaps with white edging. Alison's baby would look nice in that. She wasn't aware of the little sigh that escaped her as she thought about the baby, but Hallam glanced at her sharply, and she blushed. Surely he wasn't mind-reading again?

She turned towards him, her blue eyes hooded, her face giving nothing away. 'Did you speak?' she asked politely, and Alison giggled.

'We've been speaking for the last fifteen minutes, I should think! I know you're busy. See you!' The door closed behind her, and Pip pinned a bright smile to her face.

'I shall have to start knitting again,' she commented, avoiding Hallam's eyes. 'Primrose will be pretty. Perhaps you could give me a lift into town when you go?'

'Of course,' he agreed politely. 'When do you start?'

'Start?' She stared blankly, her thoughts full of babies.

'At the hospital,' he said, slowly and distinctly. 'Your general training.'

'Oh, that. Um, second week in May.' For a moment she'd forgotten. She wouldn't be there when Alison had her baby. But maybe it was for the best. Her small face softened as she pictured a baby in her arms, nestling up to her, its tiny mouth puckered, its hands working as it searched for its dinner . . .

'Pip.'

'Yes?' Reluctantly, she dragged herself back to reality. Dreams were for night-time. Hallam must never suspect how she felt.

'I . . . never mind.' His mouth snapped shut, and he turned on his heel, the door clashing behind him.

'Now what have I done?' she asked aloud. Whatever she did or said, she was always in the wrong.

'Hallam, I love you,' she whispered to the closed

door, then, shrugging, she started on the pile of
reports. Work, work and more work. That was the
answer. She would work until she dropped, until
her heart no longer ached for her husband. If such
a time ever came.

CHAPTER TEN

'NURSE FIELDING!'

Pip turned wearily, as Sister Flanagan's tall, imposing figure appeared in the doorway of the sluice. 'Yes, Sister?'

'Haven't you finished bed-pans yet? I want you to help Nurse Almazan with the TRPs. Do hurry up!'

Sister disappeared in a flurry of what sounded suspiciously like starched petticoats, and Pip bit her lip in annoyance. Surely she wasn't *that* slow? Whatever she did Sister Flanagan found fault with it. In some ways she reminded Pip of Hallam. *He* was never satisfied, either.

Pip really longed to work on a surgical ward, but had three months of women's medical to get through first.

Her dream had finally been realised, she had recommenced her general training, this time at St Mary's, a small hospital in the Midlands.

Hallam had helped in every way possible, Pip conceded, carefully washing her hands after she had stacked away the bed-pans. He had been kindness itself in helping her prepare for the training. Many cosy study-sessions had been spent in his den during the dark winter evenings. That was why Pip would have preferred a surgical ward first, to put her husband's teaching into practice, but she certainly needed medical experience. Sister Flanagan was known to be a good teacher, but didn't bother

much with Pip. No doubt she knew who Hallam
was and felt that Pip didn't need her help.

Life on Rushlake Ward, women's medical, was
one long round of bed-pans, temperature pulse and
respirations, and back-trolleys. Plus last offices, of
course. Most of the ladies had heart conditions,
and many of those were over-weight, so a lot of
lifting was involved. For all she was learning of
clinical medicine, Pip felt she might as well have
been an auxiliary.

She hurried to find Lulu Almazan, the third-year
student. Even senior students still had to share the
menial tasks on Rushlake. Lulu beckoned to her
from the kitchen doorway and, mystified, Pip went
over. 'No TRPs yet? Sister said I had to help you.'

'I'm just going to start, but there was a phone-
call for you. I overheard Sister say you couldn't be
disturbed when you were working.'

Pip's eyes lit up. 'Was . . . was it . . . I mean, did
she say who it was?' Could it be Hallam to see if
she was all right? Oh, please let it be Hallam!

'No. I heard her mutter to Staff that she didn't
know what the hospital was coming to. "Personal
calls now." ' Nurse Almazan did a passable im-
personation of Sister's loud voice, and they both
laughed.

No, it could not have been Hallam then, Pip
mused as she popped the thermometer in Mrs
Young's mouth. Sister would certainly not dare to
tell *him* he couldn't speak to his wife! He had telephoned only once in the two months since she'd
left. That was during their preliminary training, the
Introductory Block, when Pip was still living in the
old and rather shabby Nurses' Home. His voice
had been warm, full of concern lest she not be set-

tling in. Just-remembering now brought a lump to Pip's throat, and she blinked rapidly to rid herself of the tears that began to well up.

To reassure him, she'd said gaily that she was having a fabulous time, simply wonderful, and was enjoying every minute. He had merely said how pleased he was, then abruptly rang off. And Pip had spent that night crying for him.

She cried a lot at nights, and was bitterly ashamed of herself for her weakness—she, tough little Pip, actually crying! It was Melanie who was the weaker, more sensitive sister.

Perhaps it was Melanie who had phoned. Pip wrote to her sister often now. Apart from filling in the blank hours when she could not sleep, she was keen to know how Melanie and Peter were getting on. And little Simon, too, of course. He was nearly three now and growing every day, according to his proud mother. A new baby was on the way, Melanie had written in her last letter.

Automatically, Pip went along her side of the ward, popping thermometers in mouths, taking pulses, counting respirations, smiling, exchanging a word here and there with the ladies, but they were getting only half a nurse for once. Hallam's baby. Wouldn't that be nice? First Alison, now Melanie. Must be something in the Surrey air, Pip thought, a tiny smile plucking at her soft mouth.

It was difficult to count respirations. Once a patient knew the nurse was trying to do just that, the pattern of breathing altered. It wasn't deliberate, but it made the job a little harder. Pip was beginning to know now when respirations were normal.

She lingered at the last bed, where old Mrs Evans

sat up, supported by a back-rest and five pillows. Her wheezing respirations were far from normal. Pip liked the old lady and, because she never had visitors, always tried to spare a moment from the busy day to cheer her up. A little smile, a few cheerful words cost nothing. And she knew Mrs Evans appreciated it. Indeed, she was a favourite with most of the nurses.

Pip paused, trying to think of something encouraging to say. But outside the rain poured down. For July, it was a bitterly cold and windy day, and everywhere was grey.

'I still hear the birds of a morning, Nurse.' Mrs Evans's wheezy voice broke into Pip's sombre thoughts. 'But autumn is coming. The summer birds will soon fly away,' she observed, her shrewd blue eyes on Pip, who paled visibly.

'Yes, so they will!' Pip trilled. 'It must be hard for them, out there in the cold and rain, though. Never mind, tomorrow might be hot!' Pip was determined to be cheerful. No-one must guess her heartache, her secret sorrow. If only Hallam cared!

Somehow the day passed. Because Pip wasn't supposed to know about the telephone call she couldn't ask Sister who had called, and left the ward at nine-thirty, still wondering. It must have been Melanie. She wasn't on the telephone or Pip could have rung to find out. Never mind, worrying and wondering would give her something to do!

She led a very full social life when she wasn't working or studying. St Mary's had a flourishing social club, and there were various societies. In addition, there was a small and very new amateur dramatic club, and staff often performed plays and shows for the patients and other staff. Pip was due at rehearsals next morning. She had a part in an Edwardian comedy. Her beautiful red hair had been much admired, and one of the nurses had lent her a hair-piece in a similar shade, so Pip was going to be the 'girl with parasol' in one sketch. Her delicate colouring and stunning hair were well set off by the pale-grey costume and pretty blue and white parasol.

She threw herself into every activity she could, not because she was extrovert, but simply to leave her less time for brooding. Yet each night that was exactly what she did. Even when she managed to drift off to sleep, it was an uneasy sleep, punctuated by dreams, mainly of a tall, dark man hovering by her bed. She would wake shivery and frightened, to find herself quite alone. No-one was standing by her bed. Yet the dream was a vivid one. The man did not have Hallam's features but those stormy eyes were his. Was there to be no escape?

Angus Sinclair was waiting for her next morning as she approached the conference room for rehearsals. He was a third-year student, but somewhat older than the others. In his late twenties, Pip judged. He had heard 'the call' as he put it, in his teens, and had gone off to somewhere in Africa to assist his missionary uncle. Now he was very nearly due to take his nursing Finals, then would probably go back to spreading the Word. He and Pip had struck up a firm friendship. Angus, a big handsome Scot, didn't have much time for girls, though he had an outgoing personality and was never short of partners. Pip assumed he felt safe with her because she was married. She made no demands on him and he made none on her.

Occasionally she tried to play Cupid, for Angus

was such a dear and she wanted him to be settled, but so far he had evaded Cupid's arrow. Probably he was happier that way, Pip mused, pausing at the hall porter's lodge just outside the hall, as she always did. Sometimes there was a letter from Melanie or Alison and, on one occasion, from Aunt Norah Tester. Look what Cupid's arrow has done to me! she reflected, waiting her turn as the porter dealt with someone else's mail.

'Message for you, Nurse.' Albert, the cheerful little porter, looked up.

'For me?' It must be Melanie, then, but if only . . .

'Telephone call from your sister. Could you phone her. See, I took the number. Said you didn't live in and I couldn't get hold of you.'

Thanking him, Pip was about to go in search of a telephone, but Angus still hovered uncertainly, and she gave him a warm smile.

'Ah, Spring has sprung, young Philippa!' he chuckled. 'Venus smiles!'

'Don't be daft! I have to ring my sister. It might be urgent,' she explained. 'Will you tell them I'll be a few minutes late for rehearsal?'

'Half of them aren't here yet. I'll walk you to the telephone. By the time we get back, the stage manager might have arrived.'

Pip was puzzled about the telephone number. No way could Melanie afford a telephone and the number wasn't one Pip knew. Could it be the Vicarage?

No, it wasn't the Vicarage, for the village postman's wife answered the phone. 'I'll get Melanie for you. Proper tizz she's in!' Mrs Durrant's cheerful voice was replaced by a whining, tearful one

Pip scarcely recognised.

'Melanie? Is that you?'

'Yes, it's me!' Melanie wailed. 'It's so awful! I just don't know where to begin.'

Pip went cold. 'Simon? Melanie, is it Simon? Something's happened?'

'No!' Melanie shrieked down the telephone. 'It's me! You always did fuss over him, but this time your sister needs you!'

When did my sister *not* need me, Pip thought wryly. 'Are you ill then?' she asked gently. Melanie sounded on the verge of hysteria, but she always over-dramatised things.

'No, but I'm leaving Peter. I can't stand him another day,' Melanie whimpered. 'It's no use you arguing with me,' she went on stubbornly.

'I'm not arguing, Melanie. It's your life, not mine,' Pip assured her calmly.

There was a stricken silence at the other end. 'You don't mean you're going to let me suffer alone!' Melanie sounded shocked, and Pip longed to shake her.

'I am in the Midlands, you are in Surrey. What can I do?'

'Well . . .' Melanie's voice trailed off miserably, then she started sobbing, and Pip tried to harden her heart but failed utterly. 'It can't be as bad as that, Melanie. What has he done, anyway?'

'Oh, I don't know. He's drinking again. Says he doesn't want another baby! How could anyone be so hateful?' Melanie cried.

Because pregnant women were over sensitive, Pip knew Melanie was making more of the situation than it warranted. It was probably just a tiff and by the time Pip got there everything would be back to normal. *If* Pip got there, she said, silently having an argument with herself.

'Perhaps you need a good night's sleep, Melanie. Could Mrs Durrant take Simon for a couple of days? Let you have a rest? It would give you a chance to talk things over with Peter, too.'

Melanie could be as stubborn as Pip when she liked, and this was one of those times. 'Peter and I have nothing to talk over,' she said firmly, and Pip sighed.

'What do you expect me to do then? I can hardly talk to him if . . .'

'That's it!' Melanie interrupted. 'Talk to Peter. Tell him how desperately ill he's making me. Please, Pip?'

Pip, still undecided, was about to protest further when Melanie went on: 'It's making Simon ill, too. He lies awake at night because I do. He's getting very thin,' Melanie hurried on, and Pip's heart sank.

Emotional blackmail. The last time her heart had stirred with pity for Simon, she had changed jobs—and landed herself with the autocratic Hallam Fielding! What mess would she land herself in this time?

Tomorrow and Friday were her days off. She *could* take a train first thing tomorrow. She was on late duty today and again on Saturday. But who would put her up? Not Melanie, that was for sure. Hallam?

But Hallam never contacted her these days. Apart from that first, brief telephone call, he hadn't bothered. Yet Pip wrote dutifully once a fortnight, just a brief page or two, to be sure. In it she chronicled her duties, what she was studying, the various disorders she'd seen, what she was doing in her off-duty . . . *That* was unwise, perhaps, but she didn't want Hallam to know she was pining for him. She had her pride. That Hallam might genuinely care for her and be hurt to know about her social goings-on, she never for one moment thought. He had Vanessa, he certainly did not need his young, immature wife. Hadn't he said so to his brother. 'I wish I had never met her.' Pip recalled the words with painful clarity.

Could she stay with Hallam? Just for her days off? Might not Vanessa be there? Unspoken and unanswered questions ran around her head until she felt it must burst.

Melanie and Simon needed her. She would pop down, see what she could do. The question of accommodation could safely be left for a while.

Melanie's relief was touching, and Pip felt better as she replaced the receiver. She mentioned briefly to Angus that her sister had problems and that she would have to go home the following day. To her surprise, he offered to drive her.

'But you can't! I mean, were you going that way?'

'No, but I'm off tomorrow. Just the one day, unfortunately. I should enjoy a drive down to soggy Surrey!' he assured her.

'It isn't *that* soggy!' she retorted smilingly. 'Are you sure, though? I . . . I don't know where we can stay,' she faltered, and saw his quizzical look before he had time to hide it. Angus knew her husband lived in Surrey. Naturally he would assume she would stay there. Pip flushed, then abruptly changed the subject. Having Angus there would make this more difficult, but a lift would mean she wouldn't need to spend the whole day travelling.

Next day, the gales almost blew them down to Surrey, and they were at their destination well before lunch.

Pip decided to call on Mrs Durrant first, supposing that Melanie was staying there, but the postman's wife assured her Melanie had gone off the previous afternoon, taking Simon with her.

Pip's heart missed a beat. Had Peter locked her in? It wouldn't be the first time. That must be it, Melanie and Simon were imprisoned in their own home!

Put like that, it *did* sound melodramatic, and Pip smiled to herself. She was beginning to think like her sister.

'I did hear her mention someone called Hallam,' Mrs Durrant ventured, her hazel eyes anxious.

'Hallam?' Pip repeated.

'Yes. I think that was the name. Said he would take her in. Would that be Mr Fielding the surgeon?'

Pip nodded, numbly.

'Your husband, would that be?' Mrs Durrant went on.

Pip nodded again. 'Yes, I expect he's let her have a room for a day or two. I'll call there. Thank you for all your kindness, Mrs Durrant.' Pip managed a smile, but Mrs Durrant's thoughts were busy.

'I expect you *would* call there, Nurse. Him being your husband and all,' the woman persisted, her eyes glistening.

Pip felt herself redden. She'd done it again! Letting others see that she didn't go home on her days off. 'Yes, but . . . but I wanted to see what I could do for my sister first,' Pip went on, heartily.

She hurried away, then her footsteps slowed. She would have to see Hallam after all. It was unbearable. How could she settle her sister's problems, smile politely at Hallam, then calmly go all the way back to the hospital? She couldn't! She loved him to distraction. Seeing him again, so briefly, would be rubbing salt into her wounded, bleeding heart.

Pip hardly knew what to say to Angus, sitting so patiently behind the wheel of his car. 'I'm sorry. About . . . about all this driving around,' she said, her blue eyes fixed on him in unconscious appeal.

He chuckled. 'Don't worry, Pip. I'm enjoying the scenery. You're the young sister I had once.'

Pip felt a lump come into her throat. Angus had a sister who had died of polio some years before. She would have been twenty now, only a little younger than Pip. Brother and sister had been very close, Angus had told her.

'I don't know what I would have done without your help,' she whispered, then gave him directions to her own home—*Hallam's* home, she corrected herself.

The house shone in the sunlight. Flowers swayed and danced in the front garden of White Gables— the roses, particularly. It was a homecoming. They were dancing because they were pleased to see her, Pip thought wistfully.

Hallam would probably be at the clinic, he . . .

'There's a big car.' Angus pointed out the Rolls that Pip hadn't noticed.

'Oh, yes. That's his showpiece! But he often uses the sports-car. I expect he's out.'

Then Simon came hurtling down the steps and Pip swept him up in her arms. From his chatter she gathered that Mummy and Uncle were in the house.

Angus elected to sit in his car and, thankfully, Pip hurried indoors. Yes, Mummy and Uncle *were* in the house. They were in Hallam's study, and his arms were around Melanie's slender shoulders.

As Pip watched, not wanting to interrupt when Hallam was obviously comforting his sister-in-law, Melanie turned her face up to his. Hallam's lips gently brushed her cheek as Pip stood rooted to the spot. *That* didn't seem all that brotherly!

Jealousy pulsed through her blood, but she managed to overcome it and even produced a smile from the depths of her misery. She nervously cleared her throat, and the pair swung round. Hallam seemed embarrassed and Pip's smile slipped for an instant. So, when it wasn't Vanessa it was Melanie, was it?

'Pip!' Melanie, at least, was glad to see her, and the sisters embraced. Pip kept her face averted from Hallam's searching gaze. She couldn't look at him. She couldn't!

'I think Melanie's problem has sorted itself out,' Hallam said, as he gently disentangled Melanie.

Pip bit her lip. 'I . . . I'm glad. I needn't have come, then? You . . . you didn't need any help,' she blundered on. 'I'll go back. If you're sure everything is all right?' She turned anxious eyes on Melanie, who nodded tearfully.

'Yes, Hallam has sorted things out for me,' she assured Pip. 'I'm going to make a new beginning.'

A new beginning. With Hallam? Oh, no! Varied emotions chased across Pip's small face, then she nodded dully. 'I hope you'll be very happy, Melanie. Both of you.'

She turned to go, glad that Angus was there to

drive her away from the scene of her torment, then she straightened. What sort of wife was she, letting her sister steal the man she loved? If a husband was worth having, he was worth fighting for!

When she turned back from the door, determined to do battle for her husband, she saw that he was alone. 'Where has Melanie gone?' Defiantly, she stood there, chin up, head held proudly.

To her surprise, Hallam began to chuckle. 'You seem ready to do battle, Pip! Who are you going to war with? Me?'

'I . . .' She shook her head. If Melanie wanted a cheap affair, let her have one. Hallam would still be *her* husband. Perhaps he would realise how much he needed his wife by his side. Give him time to get the beautiful, frail Melanie out of his system first.

'Pip, come here.'

Startled, she was about to protest, but a consultant's command had to be obeyed. Slowly and reluctantly, she went to meet him, stopping just within his reach, and his long, powerful arms did the rest. She was cradled to his chest before she knew where she was, Hallam's hands were soothing her, stroking her hair, his voice was murmuring soft words of love.

Love? She put her hands on his chest, trying to push him away. 'Stop it! You don't love me! It's . . . it's Mel and Vanessa and . . .' She stopped abruptly as his lips met hers.

Neither spoke for some time. Hallam gazed down at her, his eyes no longer stormy-grey, but soft and tender and filled with love. 'I *do* love you, Pip. Not Melanie or Vanessa, or Sister Farrell!' he laughed, cuddling her closer. 'Seeing Melanie's distress over her husband reminded me that I had a wife. I *need* you, Pip. But there, I haven't the right to expect you to stay with me—a man old enough to be your father.'

'You're not! Old, I mean. Hallam!' Pip nestled closer, then stood on tiptoe, to try to kiss away his doubts.

An amused voice broke in just as Hallam's head bent towards her, and they moved apart guiltily.

'I hate to interrupt, but is there any chance of lunch before I drive back?' Angus lounged in the doorway, a big grin on his face, and Pip beamed at him.

'Hallam,' she began, 'this is my dear friend, Angus. He . . .'

'So I see,' her husband said coldly. All the warmth and love had disappeared without trace, leaving only the old familiar consultant, and Pip wanted to cry.

'No, please! It isn't like that. Angus gave me a lift down.'

'That was good of him,' Hallam commented drily, then held out his hand as Angus approached.

The men shook hands while Pip nervously performed the introductions. This was terrible! Just when it seemed as if all her dreams were coming true. Now Hallam believed she had a boyfriend dangling on a string!

'Naturally you must both stay to lunch,' Hallam said, courteously, just as if Pip, too, was a visitor. 'I'll see about it.'

Pip stared at the study-door as it closed noisily behind him, then turned her anguished eyes on Angus.

'I think I'd better go, Pip.' And when she would have argued, Angus went on firmly: 'It seems to me you are the one with a domestic crisis, not your sister. I'll grab a meal in town. Have you enough money for your train fare back, if you need it?'

'Yes, thank you,' she whispered. 'But . . .'

The door closed quietly behind the gentle Angus, and Pip was alone again, her world in ruins.

Hallam was in his consulting-room. When Pip found him he was sitting on the examination couch, long legs swinging idly, head bent as if deep in thought.

Pip flung herself at his feet and sat cross-legged on the cold floor, one hand clutching his immaculately-clad leg. She leaned her red-gold head against his leg, and waited. Would her love be enough to break down his suspicions? Was it possible that they *could* make a go of it?

'I have a new job for you, Pip,' he said at last, and her thin frame tensed, prepared to do battle if he wanted to send her away.

'Yes?' she breathed, frightened in case she broke the spell.

'It's poorly paid,' he went on soberly. 'The hours are long and unpredictable, the work sometimes boring. The boss is an impossible slave-driver, the accommodation isn't anything to write home about. And,' he paused dramatically while hope began to surge through Pip, 'worst of all, you will have to share a room!'

'Oh, yes, please!' Pip sprang to her feet, and launched herself at Hallam, who chuckled as he drew her into his embrace.

'Pip, Pip. We've wasted so much time, my dear. I've been a proud, selfish fool!' he murmured, as he began to kiss her hair.

'No, it was all my fault,' Pip began.

'Oh, all right. If you insist!' he laughed, and Pip laughed with him.

'I came to the conclusion that if you are difficult to live with, my dear, you are impossible to live without!' he said, huskily. 'I would have come up to see you, but you had so set your heart on nursing that it would have been selfish of me to tell you I needed you more.'

'I need you, too,' she breathed. 'But Vanessa . . .'

'Yes?'

'She kept saying she was your mistress. And you kept defending her,' Pip wailed. 'She was hateful to me!'

'I understand that now, Pip. Don't worry, Vanessa won't bother you again. She's found a rich husband, which is what she wanted.'

Pip sighed happily. The serpent had been banished from Eden! 'But you told Geoffrey you wished you had never set eyes on me,' she recalled, pain piercing her again.

'Only because I loved you and thought you were only pretending, my darling,' he assured her.

'And you kept taking Vanessa out,' she went on, in a small voice. 'And she said she was still your mistress.'

'I never invited Vanessa out once we were married, my dear. Though she often managed to turn up!' Hallam went on, ruefully. 'And she was never my mistress. I hope I have better taste! You'll take the job, then?' he teased, his eyes full of desire, and Pip nodded shyly. 'You can still carry on with your training,' he assured her, kissing her pert little nose. 'But down here, where I can keep an eye on you. Is that what you want to do?'

'Um. I *would* like to qualify. If nothing interesting happens to prevent me!' she murmured dreamily.

Then his dark head bent towards hers and nothing else mattered.

Look out for these three great Doctor Nurse Romances coming next month

THE GAME IS PLAYED
by Amii Lorin

Beautiful, brilliant and aloof, Dr Helen Cassidy has promised herself never again to be hurt by a man. Can Marshall Kirk's ruthless pursuit – and his considerable charm – make her change her mind?

DOCTOR IN PLASTER
by Lisa Cooper

When Dr Scott Sutcliffe is injured in a car accident, Nurse Caroline Hurst has to cope with a very demanding private case. But when she realises her exasperating patient has stolen her heart, how can Caroline possibly stay?

A MATCH FOR SISTER MAGGY
by Betty Neels

Maggy was an exceptionally tall girl, but that didn't prevent her from having all the emotions of a more petite woman – as she found when she fell so unrewardingly in love with Dr Paul Doelsma.

<u>Two</u> more Doctor Nurse Romances to look out for this month

Mills & Boon Doctor Nurse Romances are proving very popular indeed. Stories range wide throughout the world of medicine – from high-technology modern hospitals to the lonely life of a nurse in a small rural community.
These are the other two titles for November.

THE DOCTOR'S DECISION
by Elizabeth Petty

When Staff-Nurse Anna Forster meets the new Senior Surgical Registrar at the Calderbury Royal she realises that most clouds *do* have a silver lining. It is love at first sight for Anna, but is it the same for Paul Keslar?

NURSE RHONA'S ROMANCE
by Anne Vinton

Rhona was disappointed, though not heartbroken, when her romance with Chris Willson came to nothing: all the same, she was glad to have her work as a district nurse to take her mind off things. And she was even more thankful for her career when her next romance, with Dr Alex Denham, crashed to disaster.

On sale where you buy Mills & Boon romances

The Mills & Boon rose is the rose of romance